MAN IN TWO CAMPS

Wade Chisholm, tall and lean with a rich, dark complexion, has the bearing of a military officer, but moves with the catlike grace of an Apache. He has deep respect for his heritage, yet will raise his rifle against it. He is a man of two worlds, constantly torn by gut loyalties. And when the U.S. Government decrees the Apaches must be uprooted from their hunting grounds and moved to reservations, Wade Chisholm is forced to ride into the most important—and dangerous—assignment of his life!

MAN IN TWO CAMPS

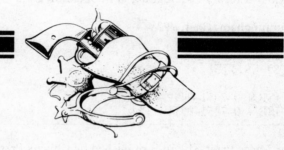

Chet Cunningham

ATLANTIC LARGE PRINT
Chivers Press, Bath, England.
Curley Publishing, Inc.,
South Yarmouth, Mass., USA.

Library of Congress Cataloging in Publication Data

Cunningham, Chet.
   Man in two camps / Chet Cunningham.
      p.   cm.—(Atlantic large print)
   ISBN 1–55504–900–1 (lg. print)
   1. Large type books.   I. Title.
[PS3553.U468M3 1989]
813′.54—dc19   89–30257
                                               CIP

British Library Cataloguing in Publication Data

Cunningham, Chet, *1928–*
   Man in two camps
   I. Title
   823′.914 [F]

   ISBN 0–7451–9499–0
   ISBN 0–7451–9511–3 Pbk

This Large Print edition is published by Chivers Press, England, and Curley Publishing, Inc, U.S.A. 1989

Published by arrangement with Donald MacCampbell, Inc

U.K. Hardback ISBN 0 7451 9499 0
U.K. Softback ISBN 0 7451 9511 3
U.S.A. Softback ISBN 1 55504 900 1

CHAPTER ONE

WEARING ONLY THE WIND

Wade Chisholm sat on a windy shelf of granite deep in the Superstition Mountains, far from any Roundeye trail, where the hawk soared, the eagle screamed, and mountain goats leaped at play. He sat where only the Chiricahua could climb.

Chisholm let the warm September sun steep into his back. It would keep him warm when the moon came and chased away the sun. He stared into the shimmering heat of the September afternoon and remembered his mother, remembered his first twelve years as a Chiricahua, how he ran with the tribe, played with the other children, learned early to bear abuse because he was different.

'Roundeye! Roundeye, Roundeye, Roundeye,' they chanted at him until he often ran home to his father and asked him what the older boys meant.

Big Red Chisholm was a mountain of a man, with a flaming red beard and red hair. He stood a head taller than any other man in camp, and could out think, out hunt, out hike and out fight any brave in their tribe. He had won the right by combat to become a Chiricahua, to take a wife, to live in camp, as

1

well as the right not to take part in the war parties and raiding bands who foraged for food, horses and sometimes women. Big Red Chisholm was a miner and he knew there was gold in the Superstitions. He aimed to find it.

Wade's father would swing him high in the air and catch him when he fell, then sit down and tell him that the other boys were jealous because he was different, because they were all of Chiricahua blood, while Little Red had hair like his father, and was half Roundeye like his father. Someday he would be the chief of them all because he would grow strong and tall and brave, and because of all this the other boys made fun of him. They were jealous.

Wade's mother was Blue Feather, the bride his father had chosen when he took a squaw. She had been as graceful as a newborn fawn, he remembered, so young and happy and contented.

Wade looked at the rocks beside him. The elders would come soon. He knew it would be today, it was the seventh day. They would come and he could talk with them. It had to be, for he was Chiricahua, and he must be purified before he could sit at the table of the council, or smoke the pipe or sit around the campfire with the elders of the tribe and counsel with them. He was Chiricahua, yet he was also Roundeye.

The elders would question him. They

would ask why he lived with the Roundeye. Why did he lead the Pony Soldiers? Why did he seek to destroy his own people?

Then his real struggle would begin. Then he would try to make them understand that the old ways were no more. The olden times when Apaches of all tribes could wander from the great river on the east to the great salt marsh of the northwest, to the towering mountains on the north and deep into the land of the Spanish talkers, was gone forever. The new times were here.

At least, he would try to explain.

A branch snapped behind him.

Wade did not move. Another branch broke to his right rear. He remained seated. A third branch broke on the other side behind him and he lifted both hands to show he was unarmed.

'Welcome to the lair of the eagle, oh wise one,' Wade said. 'It is good that you come.'

He turned then and saw the two elders seated cross-legged where he knew they would be. Each carried a lance and could have killed him with a quick thrust, but now he saw that the blades were pointing to the rear. He was welcome.

'Little Red Feather, we welcome you. It is time for you to come to the camp by the bubbling spring. We need you at our council.'

Speaking was One Horse Thunder,

3

medicine man for this band of Chiricahuas. He had seen many moons, traveled the trails of the Apache, and guided them with the great spirits.

'Did you dream?' One Horse Thunder asked Wade.

Wade nodded. 'A screaming eagle came to me,' he said. 'The eagle landed on my shoulder and spoke to me, but I couldn't understand his words. Then it rained and the thunder spoke to me but again I did not know what it was saying. Yes, I have dreamed, but I am not sure what the dreams meant.'

Wade stumbled as they walked. He had not eaten for three days, and had only a few sips of water. One Horse held up a gourd and gave him water, sweet and pure and still cool from the Salt River far below.

They walked for two hours until they were off the high places, and near the stream. Walking left Wade giddy and unsure of his steps. One Horse stopped by the water and sat cross-legged looking into the chattering of the stream here high in the mountains. The other elder quickly prepared dry sticks and took a coal from his metal box and started a fire. Wade had never seen that done before, but he was too weak to comment. On the fire One Horse brewed a broth for him.

Wade drank the bitter tasting liquid and almost at once felt better. They rested there for an hour and when they moved again Wade had most of his strength back.

Two hours more of walking and they came to the canyon of the bubbling springs. It was far north of the Salt River cave, up somewhere near the inception of the Salt River or the tributary they followed. Soft green trees filled the little valley, and water bubbled up from the ground and it was sweet and pure.

The sun was down, dusk was near. In the half light Wade saw the summer camp, no permanent shelters, no tepee or hogans, only small campfires and sleeping mats. At the far end of the little valley a good sized fire burned, it was for the council. Wade wished that he could have some sleep before he spoke with the elders. His mind still was not clear. But he had spent his seven days on the bluff. He had welcomed the sun and the moon. He had listened to the thunder and had seen lightning jab at the peaks around him. He had met with the cool rain in the evening, and seen the wind blowing in all its force. He was cleansed, his soul was free to seek the great spirit, to reason with the elders, to be a Chiricahua again.

The cry of the coyote echoed through the camp and the elders all left their work and moved to the council fire. The elders wore their robes of fur, some buffalo, one of bear to prove his strength, several of finely chewed doeskin. Only Little Red Feather had no

5

robe. He sat with the other chiefs and elders around the small council fire, fed now with only dry, seasoned wood so the smoke was light and would not hide anyone across the circle.

One Horse Thunder rose and danced slowly around the circle, his dance descriptive of past glories of the tribe, but not as vigorous as it once was. When he was sure he had gained the attention of the spirits, he returned to his place slightly in front of the others near the fire.

'Little Red Feather is a Chiricahua again,' One Horse said. 'He has forsaken the ways of the Roundeyes and returned to the clan. He has spent seven days and seven nights on the wishing and dream rocks. He is cleansed.'

There was a murmur of approval from the elders.

'The stench of the Roundeye is gone from him, he has returned to the council of his own free will. He will speak his own mind to us.'

Chisholm sat, cross-legged like the others, staring at the fire. Now that he was here, suddenly he did not know what to say. All the words he had prepared, all of the reasons, the logical arguments, the Roundeye reasons deserted him.

'Brothers,' he began. 'It is true, I am cleansed. I have spent my seven days and seven nights on the dream rocks. The last three days no food passed my lips. And I did dream, but I do not understand the dream. I will tell you of it soon.'

He stopped and stared around the circle. Twelve men. Four of them he ran with as children, boys who teased and taunted him. Three more he had known as elders when he was a boy. This was a combined band of three or more, joined now to continue the old ways.

'I must speak plainly, the old ways are dead, they are gone, the old ways will never be our ways again.'

'No, no, it cannot be!' The angry shout came from Broken Lance, a warrior only two years older than Wade, one of the men from his former band who openly had carried a dislike for the Roundeye. Now he stood to continue, but One Horse Thunder lifted his hand sharply, slanting his open palm upward toward Broken Lance. It was the sign of the medicine man that the order of things were not right. It was the firmest sign of disapproval that could be invoked.

Broken Lance stared at One Horse Thunder, the sign was repeated, and slowly he sat down where he had been.

Wade continued. 'I must speak plainly. That was part of the meaning of my vision. I know you have called me Two-Man, and for some it was an insult. I am Two-Man, I have a leg in both camps, I know how the Chiricahua think, I also know how the Roundeyes think and what they do and what

7

the Pony Soldiers do and how they think.

'All this must be considered by each of you when I say, I know the old ways of the Apache, the old ways are dead. Think back to the old days with me. Remember the long hunting trips? Remember chasing the buffalo to the north, ranging far to the salt marshes, to the northwest? Remember how the Superstition Mountains, as the Roundeyes call them, were unapproachable by anyone but an Apache? Remember when we could always get on our horses and ride into Mexico when things did not go right here in the Roundeye lands?

'The Roundeyes call us nomads, we wander from place to place, we call no land our own, yet we want to keep all of it for ourselves. We watch the Roundeye move into our hunting grounds, into our lands and build houses and start towns, and put up fences to keep us out and his cattle and horses in. The Roundeye owns land. He has *property*.' Wade looked around the circle. Some of the younger men knew and understood the idea of owning land, the older men still refused to discuss it. They claimed the Apache, the Chiricahua, owned all the lands he used to hunt on and to live on.

'I am Two-Man, with a foot in each camp. I say the old ways are gone. It is truth because we no longer can ride for two days in any direction and find only Apache. We find

Roundeyes, their women and their children, their houses, their cattle and their fences. It is not that I say the old ways are dead, each of you in his heart can see the changes, each of you knows that things are not as they were even ten years ago, or twenty or thirty. Your own heart will tell you I speak the truth.

'You know of Bull Elk, the chief and medicine man of one band of our brothers. Bull Elk has seen the signs in the desert and in the mountains. He has sat on the dream rock and at last he came to a decision. Soon he will take his people out of the mountains, will put down his guns, and will go with the Pony Soldiers to the new home of the Chiricahua.'

'Never a prison! Never a reservation!' It was Broken Lance, who jumped to his feet. He did not look at the medicine man. He glared at Wade, and slowly pulled his knife from his robes.

'Roundeye, you are a disgrace to your beautiful mother. You are a devil who desecrated the dream rocks. I challenge you, now in the Chiricahua way. We will fight with knives in the circle with the cloth between our teeth. We will see if the Roundeye stench is gone from the so called Chiricahua or if the stink is even more strong!' Broken Lance turned and stalked away from the fire.

Everyone looked at One Horse. He sighed, stared into the fire, then rose slowly.

9

'The challenge has been made. Honor is at stake. There will be a fight in two days. There must be time for preparation, and meditation.'

Still everyone sat where they had been.

Wade caught the medicine man's glance.

'May I continue? I may not have the chance to speak what my heart tells me again, especially if Broken Lance is as good with a knife as he is with his tongue.'

One Horse looked at each of the elders and sub-chiefs in turn. No one turned his face away. One Horse nodded.

Wade put his mind away from the challenge, and thought only of his reasons for coming back to the blanket. He looked at each of the tribal elders in turn, thanking him with his eyes for the patience and understanding. Then he began, and he talked for two hours, setting out all of his reasons why the Chiricahuas must not fight the white man, that they must learn how to live in harmony with the Roundeyes just as they did with the rattlesnake, the cold winters and the time of the long drought.

At last he finished. There were no questions. They would come from each of the elders between now and the fight, and he would answer each one from his heart, trying to convince each that the old ways were dead, but a new way would be just as good.

Little Red Feather spent the night in the

soft grass behind a downed tree. For a time he listened to the chirping of the katydids. A night hawk called and he heard a night-feeding rabbit moving about. So gentle, so at peace. There was a lot to say for the Apache way, and he would try to preserve what he could of it for as long as he could. But one thing he was sure of, the Apache Chiricahua and the Pony Soldiers must never fight again. At last he went to sleep with that thought on his mind.

The next day was devoted to gaining back the strength he had lost in the fasting. He ate berries and freshly roasted rabbit. He had cakes made of ground corn and then gorged himself on fresh venison that had been brought to camp by one of the hunters. All during this time the elders came to him, spoke quietly, asking him how the red man and the Roundeye could live together.

Chisholm spoke of many ways and each time he mentioned a reservation, the old men's eyes turned sad and lost whatever sympathy they had built up for the idea. At least he had made a start, Wade decided. He could go back to the army headquarters in Prescott and talk with General Crook and give him the Indian's side in the situation. George Crook would listen, he was not one of the breed of Army officers who said the only good Indian was a dead Indian.

Then Wade forgot about the reason he

11

came to the mountains. Instead he planned how he could stay alive the next morning. If he failed there, all his other work would be wasted. Wade tried to remember all he could about Broken Lance. He had known him for as long as he could remember. Broken Lance had always been one of the bigger, older boys. When he was twelve and Broken Lance was fourteen, Wade remembered that he caught up with him in height and weight and that they had wrestled one day not totally for sport. Broken Lance had suffered a bloody nose and Wade had sat on him for half the day gloating.

But Wade knew little of him since he had become a man. He was six inches shorter than Wade's six-feet two-inches. He was lean and fit, strong, Wade was sure. One thing Wade remembered about Broken Lance was his hands. He was quick, fast with a knife, axe or deadly throwing a knife. Wade was sure the Indian had honed his skills greatly in the past dozen years. He was a good example of the Chiricahua fighting machine, otherwise he would not have challenged a bigger, heavier man.

Basic Chiricahua fighting strategy: never enter a fight you know you will lose. Think long before getting into a fight you think there is a good chance you might lose.

Broken Lance thought he could win.

The sun came over the mountains the next

morning and the two men were in the clearing low in the small valley, where the stream widens out to six feet and skims over bright gravel and sand. The older boys of the tribe had used hatchets to dig a circle eight feet in diameter. A ditch two inches deep marked the area of soft, short grass.

Both men stood near the circle. They wore only loincloths, their bodies rubbed with rabbit grease so the other man could not get a good grip on an arm or thigh. The strip of soft doeskin was three feet long and four inches wide. Wade knew the rules. The doeskin must stay in the combatant's teeth at all times. Each man had one knife and he must stay inside the circle. If either man left the circle the braves would push or throw him back in.

It was a fight to the death. There could be no draws, no quarter. To give up was to die, immediately.

Wade had witnessed only one fight like this before. He was not surprised the night before to find strangers filtering into the camp. Braves from other bands of Chiricahuas had come to witness the fight. It was not a sport, but a solemn death ceremony for one of the men. It held religious connotations since one of the fighters would soon meet the Great Spirit.

In the fight Wade had seen years ago, one man was easily the victor after only two hours. He had sliced the defeated man several times, but when he cut the blade from the other man's hand and kicked it outside the ring, he had spat on the vanquished brave, turned and walked away. His flashing knife prevented the other braves from pushing the winner back into the ring. The defeated man ran, picked up his own knife and plunged it into his heart. He knew he could never stand the shame of living after he should be dead.

Now, Wade watched Broken Lance. The Indian was confident. He bent now, flexing his legs, warming up his body for the battle. Wade had already prepared, he had run four hundred yards, and felt the sweat beading on his forehead. His arms were ready. He would fight with his right hand, but the rules allowed either hand to be used or both at once if the chance came. Wade looked at the men and boys around the circle. There were forty braves as well as twenty older boys and about twenty younger boys. No women were in sight. Women were not permitted to watch men in such activities.

Stillness settled over the crowd as One Horse Thunder came into the area. He wore his sacred headdress and a short robe made of buffalo skin. His face was painted with the black of charcoal to further proclaim the seriousness of the affair. He walked to the center of the circle and stopped. Wade wiped the sweat from his forehead and moved forward. He and Broken Lance both advanced to the very edge of the circle and stopped. To enter the circle without the medicine man's headdress was to indicate a readiness to fight. Wade stared at Broken Lance. It was up to him to withdraw the challenge if it were to be done. One time Wade had seen a challenge withdrawn and the two men embraced. That was not to happen now.

One Horse Thunder stared at Wade, but he did not say a word. The medicine man looked at Broken Lance, and all knew this was the critical point. Broken Lance looked at the medicine man, then at Wade and he spat on the ground at Wade's feet.

One Horse seemed to sigh, and from his waist unwrapped the three foot long piece of doeskin. He beckoned the men into the ring, and as they stepped across the line there was a murmur from the crowd. Now there would be a fight for sure.

The medicine man gave the end of the doeskin to both the men, then from his waist took out the special knives. They were heavy, with six-inch blades, rawhide wrapped handles and a narrow steel hand protector.

'The Great Spirit does not look with favor upon this sort of death. It is wasteful. But what must be, must be.' With that final word he handed each of the men the knives, waited until they put the doeskin in their mouths.

15

He had to step out of the circle before the battle could begin. Wade had heard of some medicine men who simply sat down in the circle and stayed there until the men called off the vendetta. Not so this time. One Horse Thunder stepped out of the ring and the contest began.

Wade felt the doeskin tighten against his teeth and he saw Broken Lance begin to circle to his left. Wade countered him, slashed out with his knife, but even with his long arms he could not make contact. Wade knew you had to dart in, to advance to get within striking range, but he had been wondering about other tactics he had thought of. He tried one, jumping forward and kicking hard, the flat top of his foot crashing into Broken Lance's stomach. The surprise move gained grunts of approval from the braves. Wade felt Broken Lance sag for a moment, then the doeskin tightened again as the Indian darted forward, his knife slashing at Wade's knifehand. The blow missed as did Wade's counter blow. They circled again, watchful, waiting. Wade knew the strategy in this battle was to try to outwait your opponent, wear him down with movement, then at the critical time, attack. But Wade had no thoughts of making it a contest of endurance. He maneuvered Broken Lance to the far side of the ring, then jerked back hard with his teeth, timing it exactly when his opponent began a forward

16

movement. The combination jolted Broken Lance forward. Wade held the doeskin and dropped to his back, his feet driving upward like battering rams. Wade had considered throwing him out of the ring, instead he blocked Broken Lance's knife arm away with his left arm and dropped the Indian downward onto his upright knife. The blade drove through the bare chest, vanished into Broken Lance's flesh up to the hilt and Wade threw him to one side, pulling his blade from the body as it smashed, lifeless into the grass.

Wade stared at the lifeless hulk of the man and then at the braves around the circle. 'When you go back to your council fires, outlaw the ring fights. There are many better ways to settle arguments between men. Let the council decide, let the elders pass judgement. Killing each other is a waste as One Horse Thunder has spoken. I must go, I must purify myself because I have taken the life of a brother. Think on everything I have told you. I will return, but first I must leave you.'

Wade looked down at his blood covered hand and the bloody knife. He threw it as far as he could into the brush of the hillside. A shouting swarm of young boys scurried after it.

'No,' One Horse Thunder said. The boys stopped. 'Let the blade of death rust and rot where it has been buried. Forever more there will be no more circle fights among this band of Chiricahuas.'

Wade heard him as he ran to the stream. There he drank, then washed the blood off his hand, then scrubbed the grease off his body in the cold water with the help of the gritty sand. He lay in the water letting the tension seep out of him, and at last rolled into the grass and waited for the sun to dry his body.

When he sat up a woman knelt beside him, put down food and drink and watched him. She was Pretty Bird.

'You are Broken Lance's woman?'

She nodded.

'You have no man. Does he have a brother?'

'No.'

'Children?'

'Two.'

'You will stay in my tepee. I will tell One Horse. You will not have to beg for food.'

He ate the cold roast rabbit and berries, then he talked to the medicine man, making provisions for the woman and her children before he set out on the trail. It would take him a long day's run to get to the place where he left his horse, his guns and his clothes. He wondered if they still would be there?

CHAPTER TWO

A ROUGH PLAN

About noon of the third day after the knife
fight, Wade Chisholm rode up to the hitching
rail outside the McCurdy General store in the
village of Phoenix. He was twenty miles from
the closest part of the Superstition
Mountains. He was tired, dusty, and hot. He
tied up the bay, slapped at his dusty pants
with the brown, high-crowned hat he wore.
Wade was clean shaven now, his hair had
returned to its flaming red color after all the
berry stain had washed out of it from a few
months back, and he was ready for some
home-cooked food. He stopped a minute and
stared up the street of this roaring metropolis
called Phoenix. Perhaps a hundred structures
all together dotted the streets. The Salt River
was three hundred yards behind him. He was
sure this little burg would never amount to
anything. It would dry up and blow away and
be nothing but another idea gone wrong,
another rotting ghost town.

He pushed open the screen door and
walked into the store. Josh McCurdy glanced
up from where he was pulling a dried prune
from a 25-pound keg he had just opened.

'Well, consarn, look what the wind just

19

blowed in,' Josh said.

'Josh, you old sidewinder. You snaggle another prune from that keg and the owner of this rat trap is gonna come gunnen' for you.'

Josh held out his hand and Wade grabbed it.

'Well, I got the rough plans laid out for the school.' He looked at Wade. 'You do remember about the school, don't you, Mr. Board of Directors President Wade Chisholm?'

'That one I remember, Josh. I'm not ever going to forget. Before we get to that, you got anything good to drink in here? I mean anything!'

'Sounds like you dried out a mite up there in the hills.' Josh took out a pair of glasses and motioned Wade into the stock room just behind the counter. From a shelf he took down a bottle labeled 'Premier Whiskey.' The label claimed it had been aged in oak wood for more than five months. Wade spilled some in a glass, filled it with water from a blue pitcher nearby and took a long swallow.

'Rot your guts right out of you,' Wade said, 'but better than that local cactus whiskey you tried to make last year. Remember that God-awful stuff you made?'

'Since that's the only drinking stuff in the territory at the time I don't remember you turning any down.'

'True,' Wade said. 'Now, you've got some

20

rough plans?'

'Yep. Ralph Kleen. He's new in town, came out of Ohio where he was a carpenter and a contractor, he said. Take a look at these.'

Wade looked in surprise at the drawings Josh showed him. They were journeyman plans, to scale, with the type of construction suggested, sizes, materials needed, and even where the workmen may be recruited.

'He thinks we should go to adobe block, we can make it right here and let it cure in the sun. So we cut our costs way down on the material. He figures two story for the main building, with living quarters upstairs, the kitchen and dining room. he has it set up two ways. We can do plan "A" for 30 kids, or go to "B" to take care of 60.'

Wade looked at the plans closer and was amazed. 'These are professional plans, Josh. We couldn't get anything better in Boston or New York. Don't let this Kleen person get away. Tell him we want detailed plans which we'll pay him for, and then ask him to give you a bid for the construction. We might as well get a package deal for it. Have you thought about location?'

'Well, yep, I have. Martha talked to me about it. Her idea was that the Miller ranch was too far from town. It's almost six miles out there and she figures that's too far to do much good. Her idea is that this is where the

21

people will be, and this is where the orphans and the little Indian kids will be.'

'So what did Martha suggest, Josh?'

'Well, she figured that we should use some of the money and buy a little piece of land closer in to town, maybe just right on the edge of town and close to the river if possible.'

'Sounds reasonable. That will make it better for you too, Josh. You won't have to traipse all the way out to the ranch. Later on when the value goes up, we can sell the ranch, or even rent it out for some income for the school.'

Josh beamed.

Wade looked at the plans again. 'Josh, why don't you have this Kleen design in some living quarters for teachers. We're going to need two or three teachers, and maybe an apartment for the administrator, whether it's you or somebody else if you get tired of the job. That would balance it out nicely. Oh, let's go with the larger size, for the sixty youngsters. That should do for a few years until we need to expand.'

Josh lifted his glass. 'Here's to you, Wade Chisholm. A finer gentleman never walked this Godforsaken desert. And to the lady we're naming the school for, Hannah Miller, may the Lord rest her soul.'

'Yes, I'll drink to that,' Wade said.

A woman came in looking for some yardage

and a new frying pan, and Josh took care of her. Wade settled down in the chair and relaxed. There was a lot to say for the Apache way, but a good mattress and springs never hurt a man either. He was looking forward to a bed at the hotel and maybe even a hot bath, if there was any hot water to be had.

But when Josh came back in a few minutes later he said he and Martha wouldn't consider his going to a hotel, he would stay at their place, and they had lots of hot water.

That afternoon, Josh and Ralph Kleen met with Wade in the store and they went over the plans for the school. Kleen was a short man, lean and full of energy. He was in his late forties, and said he had been working in the city of Chicago in the water department when he decided he had dug enough ditches and laid down enough pipe to last him a lifetime.

'So here I am, trying to make a living trying to get this town moving. The water works will be easy just as soon as we get a few more people.'

They decided where the teacher units should go and the apartment for the superintendent. Then they all had a bottle of warm beer that came in on the last stage.

★   ★   ★

The next morning Wade rode out as soon as the sun was up. All the morning he thought of nothing but Hannah Miller, the girl they named the school for. The first time he saw her she had been a captive of the Chiricahua high in the Superstitions near Salt Creek cave. He had waited until the drunken party was over in the cave, then gone in and brought her out and taken her to Phoenix before the Indians realized she was gone. She had been the only survivor when a raiding party came down on the Miller ranch and looted it for everything they could carry.

He had spent several days in Phoenix and got to know Hannah and fell in love with her. Then he had to go tell General Crook in Prescott what he had learned about the Chiricahua's hideout. By the time the engagement was over with the Indians and he came back to Phoenix, he had found Hannah murdered, and three sets of tracks leading away from the door.

He had tracked down the killers and settled the score, and then decided to use money and stocks found at the Miller ranch to put up a school in her honor and memory. As One Horse Thunder said, what must be, must be.

Wade spent two days on an easy ride the 60 miles to Prescott, and reported at the headquarters of the Army of Arizona or as it was known officially as the Department of Arizona in the Pacific Military district. General George F. Crook, demoted to his temporary rank of bird colonel after the Civil

24

War, was the commander, and a personal friend of Wade Chisholm. He also worked for the man and the army as a scout.

Camp Prescott was not the most impressive military installation Wade had ever seen. The command buildings were framed with shiplap siding and two of them were painted. The officers' quarters and the enlisted quarters were made of logs hauled in from the mountains and adobe, sun-cured adobe clay bricks.

The stables were open affairs and the stock had no protection during the bitter cold winters. But September was mild this year. Wade rode into the camp, gave his mount to a soldier at the gate and went to the commander's office.

A new aide was at the desk outside the commander's office, and Wade stopped there.

'Captain, I'm Wade Chisholm. Like to see the General if he's got a spare moment.'

'Chisholm . . . I don't have anything about an appointment for you. Is it a civilian matter?'

'Reckon not, I do some scouting work for the General.'

'Well, he's busy this morning, perhaps sometime this afternoon.'

'Busy you say. Is he with someone? A meeting?'

'Sir, that isn't for you to question. The fact is he isn't, however . . .'

The captain stared in open mouthed amazement as Wade walked past him, waved and opened the door to the general's office.

Wade left the door open as he walked in, and waved. 'General, the Captain said you were busy, when should I come back?'

Col. George F. Crook laughed. 'Back, you're here so stay. I'll talk to my aide later, if he'll close the door.'

The door closed quietly.

Col. Crook chuckled. 'These new ones are always hard to break in.' He pulled at his beard. 'Well, you're back, that must mean you're ready to go to work. Have you been into the Superstitions?'

Wade told him of the meeting with the tribe, and the reactions.

'If I understand you, Wade, you're telling me that some of the older heads are willing to listen, a few might be ready to come out, but that the younger leaders are holding back.'

'That's about it. What we need is a respected chief, one of the younger or middle-aged chiefs who wants to come out and help him convince the rest of them. It looks like it will be a long struggle, General. I'd say it will be a few here, a band there, a bunch here. It all depends where the reservation is and how well it is managed. These men are hunters, they must have an area where they can hunt.'

'My boy, that is a matter for the politicians,

not the army. They have indicated to me several times to leave that matter to them. We are to bring in the Indians, they will decide where the reservations will be.'

'They are denying us the whole group of reasons we could use with the Apache. He would come out if he were given a part of the Superstitions for his reservation. If he's sent far away to the plains he knows nothing of, he will not come out. And still we know that he must come to the reservation.'

'So Chisholm, we do like always, we play the role of a good soldier and do what our commanders tell us to do.' Col. Crook spread out a map on his desk and pointed to the Superstitions.

'This is our problem. It's a vast area of different sets of mountain ranges moving all the way up to Flagstaff. The Apaches have virtual command of the whole region. That's about a 60 × 90 mile block of territory, over five thousand square miles of Arizona. One of our keys may be a chief named Medicine Basket, have you heard of him?'

'He's not a Chiricahua. He's a Jicarilla, about forty, I'd say. I've heard good things about him.'

'But he's Apache, right? One of the several clans and bands?'

'Yes, General. And many times these different bands fight among themselves, but if the Pony Soldiers drive them to the wall, they

27

will get together quickly.'

'That's just what we don't want them to do. I'll show you my grand strategy, which really is no strategy at all. Quite simply I think you can do more good with the Apaches than six or eight companies of cavalry. I don't want to slaughter these people, I want to control them. By now even some of your own people realize that times have changed. I want you to reason with them, to talk to Medicine Basket and get him to talk to more of the tribes and bands, and work out an exodus of as many Apaches as you can.'

'It will not be easy,' Wade said. 'I have nothing to promise them.'

'You can tell them I think there will be a reservation near Fort Apache, and near San Carlos, east of us, east of Phoenix. That's the best we can do, right now.'

The general stood. He wore a long beard and often twirled the tips of both sides so they stood out. He never smoked or drank, and had more compassion for the Indians than any ranking army officer of his day. Which did not set too well with his commanders, but they had no other commanders who could do as well in the field.

'Come see what I have for you to take along?' They went through a side door and along a private walk to a store house. Inside were stacks of merchandise; blankets, pots and pans, tin plates, an array of knives in all

28

sizes, and more blankets.

Crook beamed. 'What do you think? It's all for the Indians. Not trading material, but gifts to all those who agree to move to the reservation.'

'No,' Wade said.

General Crook looked up quickly.

'General, this is not the way. It sets up the wrong mood. It's like offering a trained dog a bit of meat if he does the trick. The Apache will resent the very idea. No gifts, not if I'm to go in and talk to Medicine Basket.'

General Crook had put on his ostrich-feathered dress hat for the jaunt outside, and now he stared at Wade from under the pointed front of it. His small brown eyes were stern and he stroked his beard, twisting the long strands on the right side.

'Now you see, Wade, why I want to give you those major leaves. Then I could simply order you to take the goods.'

Wade laughed. 'Yes, sir. And then I would have to report that all except the blankets were lost when the wagon crossed the Salt River. The blankets were stolen by the Chiricahua.' Wade smiled as he stared back at the general.

'Dammit, all right. Didn't you ever learn in the army not to argue against a superior's decisions?'

'Maybe that's why I'm not in the army any more, General.'

'Colonel. Wade, can't you see good?'

'We'll get that star back for you yet, General, you just wait and see.'

Crook grinned, he liked this young man. 'Is there anything you need?'

Wade thought a minute. 'I'll want a patrol camped just outside the Superstitions for messengers. If we're going to do anything it should move quickly so we can get my people out of the mountains before the snow comes.'

'You need a six man camp?'

'That should be enough.' Wade smiled again. 'Then there's one more need I have. Within the next few weeks there's a building going to be put up in Phoenix. It's to be called the Hannah Miller School, for orphans, outcasts, Indians, Mexicans, maybe even a few gringos. We sure could use two or three of your best engineers to offer help and assistance.'

Crook frowned for a moment. 'You want me to authorize Cavalry personnel . . .'

'It's a non-profit trust fund with a board of directors, and it would be good public relations for the army with the people of Phoenix.'

'I'll consider it. Anything else you need for the operation?'

'Why yes, sir. A request for Sgt. Timothy Kelly on the messenger unit.'

'I'll put him in charge of the detail. You tell them what you need them to do.' Col. Crook

30

paused. 'You've considered that offer I made you? I'll get your commission reactivated and put gold leaves of a major on your shoulder. Bring you into my personal staff. Wade, you went through West Point, and that took a lot of doing, you were a good officer for four years and reached the rank of captain. Your country could use you in the next few years. This Indian trouble is going to be going on for another ten years.'

'And I'd probably get trapped into a job pushing paper somewhere, General Crook. I haven't shut the door, but when I see the attitude of our leading generals, I get angry. Kill or hang all warriors, that's what General Phil Sheridan said. General Sherman is just as single-minded. Colonel Nelson Miles is tough but seems fair enough. I'd have to think on it for some time.'

'You think, Wade, and in the meantime go bring in about five-hundred Apache to the reservation.'

Wade thought of it, then frowned. 'I would say fifty would be a good first bite out of the Apache's pie. We'll see.'

The next morning Wade rode out from Camp Prescott with Sgt. Tim Kelly, a longtime friend, and five other troopers. All had strong horses and each man trailed a second mount. For fast courier service they would use both horses, riding one to near exhaustion, changing horses and riding the fresh one and letting the tired one rest unburdened.

Tim Kelly was all Irishman, built low to the ground, square and solid like a rick of cordwood. A broad chin, reddish brown hair and freckles on a grinning face with green eyes. He limped slightly from a bar room brawl nearly forgotten. They had hit the trail at six a.m. and would get to Phoenix slightly after noon the next day. There they would pause briefly, then go on to the base of the Superstition Mountains where the Salt River flowed out heading for Phoenix, but much of the year faded into the desert before it arrived there.

Noon of the third day they had established their camp in a little grove of cottonwoods in the flood plain of the stream and had begun work with shovels to dig out a suitable swimming hole in a bend in the stream. The troopers saw the mission as a few days on their own away from officers and away from any real duty. They would be ready on five minutes notice to get a message on the way to Colonel Crook.

Sgt. Kelly sat in the shade sipping a canteen cup of cold water from the stream.

'So, Major, I understand that we sit here on our asses until you tell us to do something. I like that kind of duty.' He paused, looking at Wade. 'Sure you don't want me and, say, two of my boys to come along? Hell, we can be quiet, hide at night, do all that Indian stuff.'

'You think so?'

'Sure, any of it,' he said wishing he hadn't.

Wade stripped off his buckskin shirt and folded it neatly.

'I'll give you a test. If you can pass it, you go along with me.'

'Fine with me.'

'See that boulder over there near the edge of the stream, the one that's about three feet high, the brownish one.'

'Yep.'

'I want you to go over there, sit beside the rock, lean into it, blend your body with the rock so it looks like you're a part of the rock.'

Kelly frowned. 'I can hug the damn thing, but I've got blue shirt and blue pants on. I'd stand out like a raw recruit on parade.'

'Oh, then you'll have to take off your clothes and rub sand into your skin until you're the same color as the rock. That's how an Apache does it. That's how an Apache can jump up in front of you when you've been looking for him. He's there but you can't see him until you're within range of his lance, or his knife.'

'Well, I guess I don't want to try to be an Apache then.' Tim looked up surprised. 'Hey, you taking off your pants too?'

Wade stripped off the buckskin pants and folded them on top of his shirt. He took a loincloth and tied it around his waist with the flaps of doeskin in front and in back, then worked his feet back into his Apache moccasins.

'I'm ready,' Wade said.

'Ready? No gun, no provisions, no horse. What the hell you mean you're ready?'

'I'm ready to go in and see the Apaches. This time I'm going as one Apache to another. I'll talk to the Chiricahua again, to the Coyotero, Jicarilla, Mescalero, and if I can find any, Mimbreno, Pinal and Tonto. We're all Apaches.'

'No food?' Tim asked.

Wade slid his hand toward his waist and turned with the sharp edge of a six-inch hunting knife resting against Tim Kelly's soft throat.

'I'll find food where I am, as any Apache would. I'll find water and warmth and people. You keep your boys here and have one of them ready to ride. I may be a day, I may be a week, and it could be two weeks. If I'm not back in two weeks, ride back and report to the general what has happened. But for God's sake, don't send in a search party looking for me.'

He put the knife away in the narrow sheath on his left hip tied to the loincloth rawhide thong.

'Now, old friend, rest, and wait. I'll be back.'

Wade Chisholm who would be known as Little Red Feather, turned and walked through the shallow Salt River toward the trail that would lead him deeper into the Superstitions and the other mountains. Deeper than he had been since he was twelve.

CHAPTER THREE

THE CHALLENGE

Wade Chisholm came to the headwaters of the Salt late that day and pushed on, into land that he could not remember walking, along trails and small streams that were strange to him. For a time he saw no evidence of inhabitants, then gradually he saw bushes stripped of berries, saw where women had dug for roots and grubs. He had eaten berries and water during the day, and as the night came he found a small ravine with trees. He scraped leaves together to form a bed and slept soundly.

His body had adjusted easily to the way of the Indian again, partly because he was young and vigorous, partly because he had willed it to adjust. He had been an Apache until he was more than twelve years, that part of his heritage could never be taken away from him. Chisholm had purposefully skirted around

35

the Chiricahuas.

He had planted the seeds with them, and he hoped that they would take root and flourish. He would see One Horse Thunder on his way back to the army detail and Sgt. Kelly.

He had heard that Medicine Basket was in the edge of the Mazatzal Mountains to the north, well past Granite Peak towards the lofty Mount Ord. Wade had never met the chief of the Jicarilla. He was about forty years old, a long time leader of the sister tribe in the Apache nation. The Apaches were made up of several tribes and many more bands that had split off and wandered on their own. They all spoke much the same language, much dotted with Spanish from their frequent south of the border visits. Medicine Basket was not old by Roundeye standards, but for the Indian, especially the hard working subsistence level of the Apache, he was well into his lifetime. Many Apaches died by the time they were forty from sickness, in battle, or simply because the hard life had used up their vitality.

Wade met the first Jicarillas the afternoon of the second day. Four women were picking berries. At first they greeted him from a distance, then when he got closer they saw he carried no bow or arrows, so he could not have been one of their hunters.

He told them he came to see Chief

Medicine Basket. They told him their last summer camp was just over the ridge near Acorn Lake. By the time he arrived there was a delegation of braves waiting for him. Ten braves lined the path on either side. They could not know who he was or where he came from. It was a greeting of the most formal kind, usually reserved for visiting chiefs.

Wade did not speak to the braves, or glance right or left at them, it was not expected. They were an honor guard and guides to the place of the chief.

The Jicarilla and Chiricahua had not fought each other for a long time, many winters, and while they were not enemies, they would not want to share the same lodge or the same hunting grounds. Now the braves did not yet know from what tribe the visitor came.

The summer camp of the Jicarilla nestled on the edge of a small lake a quarter of a mile across, near a stand of timber and wooded hills that led up to the high Mount Ord to the north. It was a good campsite, with plenty of water, graze for their horses, berries and roots to dig and the timber where hunting would be excellent. And there were no Roundeyes within many miles.

For the summer camp they had built a wickiup for their chief, under huge pine trees near the lake. It was ten feet square, solidly built with poles and covered with sections of carefully woven grass mats to keep out the wind and rain of summer.

Wade stopped a dozen feet in front of the wickiup and waited. A moment later a tall man stepped out of the open door. He was taller by a head than most of his braves, with broad shoulders, a deep chest and an intelligent face, with black eyes, large straight nose and a mouth that often curled with laughter.

It was up to the host to speak first. He looked at Wade and there was no recognition, but no suspicion either. If he noticed the flaming red hair of his guest, he did not indicate it. Such an action would be discourteous and disrespectful. There could be no doubt in the chief's eyes that he was being visited by a half-breed.

'Welcome to our camp. I am Medicine Basket, these are my people, you are as welcome as the first rains of spring, as free in our camp as the birds are to fly in the sky.'

'Thank you. I have heard much of the great Chief Medicine Basket, and I am honored that you meet me. I am Little Red Feather, I am Chiricahua. My mother was Blue Feather from the Salt River, and my father a Roundeye Big Red Chisholm. I come in peace and bring you welcome and greetings from One Horse Thunder from the Superstition Mountains.'

They talked in the wickiup. After they had sat and smoked a long stemmed pipe, both men leaned back and their faces became serious. It was time to talk.

'One Horse Thunder is talking with his elders and sub-chiefs about moving to the reservation. One Horse says he is tired of the fighting, tired of seeing his young men cut down by the rifles of the Pony Soldier. He has seen enough war and he wants a lasting peace with the Roundeye, one that will not be broken until the rocks melt.'

'One Horse permits his braves to go on raids against the Roundeye. If he did not the Pony Soldiers would not seek him out.'

'It would be good if several of the bands in the mountains could come out at the same time. The white chiefs would like that and more Apaches would have more bargaining power with the white chiefs. It is said that Medicine Basket has thought of bringing his people to the reservation at White Mountain.'

Medicine Basket closed his eyes, looked up at the hole in the top of the wickiup where the smoke escaped from the small fire ring in the center of the house.

'It is a problem that hangs heavy on my heart. It weighs me down like a small leaf trying to hold up a large rock in the lake. I know what is best for my people, but I must convince them first. It is hard to reason with the angry young bucks.'

'The old ways are dying, Chief Medicine Basket. Surely you can see the signs. The old ways are dead, new ways must come. No longer can the Apache wander over the vast lands called Arizona and New Mexico free and unhindered. When I was a boy we could wander for weeks and never see a Roundeye. Now they are everywhere like the seeds from a field of puff flowers, their tiny seeds on white wings flying into every valley, to the plains and plateaus, and soon they will be in our beloved mountains.'

'It is true.'

'Great Chief, I am half Roundeye. I lived in an Apache camp for my first twelve years. I am Apache. I am also Roundeye. After I was captured by the Pony Soldiers in a raid, I was raised in a Roundeye camp by a pony soldier. He taught me the way of the white man. He taught me to think as a white man, to live, to read and to write. He sent me to the white man's school. So I have one foot in each camp. I know the Chiricahua and Jicarilla. I know the white man. I can see the best of both sides and I hope to bring both of these great people together so all can live in peace. Is not this an honorable work?'

'Yes, Little Red Feather. It is an honorable work. I have heard of you, and your exploits with the Pony Soldiers. I also know of the moderate stand the No Star General has. He can be a friend to the Apache. But it can be so only if we help him, if we help our own people.'

'And there are those who do not wish to be helped?'

'Many, some of them with followers. One here in my own camp, Swift Fox. He is young, he is angry. He wants to go on raids as the Chiricahua do, but the elders tell him no. We will not be able to hold him long. He will strike out, take his family with him and any of the others who feel as he does.'

'He is wrong. Perhaps I can talk with him.'

'You must. We cannot go into the Roundeye reservation until all of my band agree. The wise men, and all the braves must know that this is the best way. What can I tell my people about the land where we will go? Is it the mountains? Will there be much game to hunt? Will the mescal be good there? Is there plenty of the agave leaves for our women to roast in our earthen pits?'

'I asked the No Star General the same question five sunsets ago. He could only say he was not sure. The great Chiefs in Washington have set aside four reservations, two in the land of Arizona and two in the white man's New Mexico. It will probably be to the White Mountain reservation or the San Carlos, both are to the east of here, east of the village of Phoenix. I have been to neither, I know nothing of them.'

'How can you ask us to leave the land of our fathers where we have lived for so many years and journey to a place we know nothing

41

of?'

'I ask it only to stop the killing of my people. To stop the war that the Apache can never win. The white men come like the raindrops from the sky, thousands of them. There is no stopping lightning when it is about to strike. Not even the Apache warriors can stop the thousands of Pony Soldiers who are in this land and the additional thousands who can be sent. It is simply a war that the Apaches cannot win. As with any battle, the wise Apache chief knows the outcome, and he will turn and ride away from any fight he knows he will lose. It is now time for the Apache nation to understand that the old ways are dead, that the new ways must be followed. That this is a fight the Apache cannot win, so he should not continue making new arrows.'

The two men bent forward and continued talking. When the sun stood directly over the wickiup, food was brought by two young girls. They put down the food, smiled at the visitor's red hair, then left quickly. The food came in shallow woven baskets on green leaves. Roast rabbit, chopped in half with hatchet, and flavored with salt! He saw cornmeal balls in another basket, freshly picked blackberries, and a pottery mug. Curiously he looked inside. A white fluid.

Medicine Basket watched him intently.

'Try the drink,' he said.

Wade's early training guided him. When you visit the wickiup and are offered food you drink or eat—all of it. You leave nothing for to do so indicates you do not like the food and it is an insult to your host.

Wade put the mug to his lips and tasted, then drank. His surprise could not have been greater. It was fresh milk, still warm from the cow he guessed. He drank all of the milk without putting the mug down, then smacked his lips and smiled.

'It is good that you have milk here, feed it to all the *ninos*, it will make their bones grow strong,' Wade grinned. 'You have a cow? Medicine Basket has a cow?'

'Yes, we found two wandering far away from their home, so we borrowed them and before we could butcher them someone remembered the white man's way of milking a cow, and now it is my family's cow.'

'The new ways, Chief Medicine Basket. You are already using the new ways. All the children should have milk. Perhaps you will get it on the reservation.'

'Perhaps,' Medicine Basket said, then they began eating and did not speak until the bowls and baskets were empty. The two men stood and left the wickiup, walking along the stream, then around the lake.

'I must council with my elders, and with the sub-chiefs,' Medicine Basket said. 'I will not order my people to the reservation. If I can persuade the warriors this is right, then we will be ready. It is a bad time of the seasons to be moving to a new camp.'

'You would leave soon anyway for your winter camp.'

'Yes, but we know it, we have wickiups there, we know where the foods are to keep us from starving over the winter.'

'At the reservation you will be provided meat and corn.'

'It is not good to give to a man what he should earn, what he should work for.'

'That is true.'

'We will talk, it will take many days. The Jicarilla do not like to be rushed.'

'I understand.'

Before either of them could speak again, a brave of about twenty-five winters walked directly to them. He stopped six feet away and stared at Chief Medicine Basket.

'Chief, we have an enemy in our camp,' the warrior said.

'We have no enemy in our camp, Spotted Horse.'

'He stands beside you, the Chiricahua with the head of fire. I have heard of him.'

'I will talk with you about it later, Spotted Horse.'

'Now. We will talk now. I am not a child. I know why this traitor to his tribe comes here. He is a despised and hated half-breed who works for the Pony Soldiers as scout. He

44

betrays his own people. He is a rattlesnake living among us, waiting until our backs are turned before he strikes, leading a thousand Pony Soldiers against us.'

Wade drew his knife and took a fighting stance. Spotted Horse did the same, and Medicine Basket stepped between them.

'No, put away your weapons. There will be no challenges, no fighting with an honored guest in my camp. I say no!' The chief looked at Spotted Horse until he sheathed his knife. When he turned toward Wade his blade was already put away.

'We will talk more of this at council fire tonight. Spotted Horse, as a sub-chief you will be there. I will tell our people. When the sun goes down we will talk.' Chief Medicine Basket turned back towards camp. Wade followed him staring hard at the sub-chief, who was three inches shorter than the red head, but thick of chest, with powerful arms, a narrow waist and thin strong legs laced with well developed running muscles.

As Wade passed, Spotted Horse hissed at him.

'We will meet yet over our shiny blades, do not fear.'

Wade ignored the additional threat and followed the chief back to his wickiup.

'Stay here and rest, Man In Two Camps. You will be heard at our council, then we will talk among ourselves. Then you should leave

45

our camp and return in four days.'

Wade was fed again before the council fire. He had a thick strip of dried meat which he guessed was venison, but it had been coated with some kind of seasoning as it was dried and he wasn't sure. It was delicious. Wade had taken a nap on the grass pallet, and was now refreshed, reviewing in his mind all of the reasons why the Apache must go to the reservation for their own good, to prevent complete destruction of their nation.

Wade had not estimated the number of Indians in the Jicarilla camp, but now as he moved behind Medicine Basket to the council fire close to the lake, he saw four sub-chiefs, and then elders surrounding the small ceremonial fire. He guessed about 50 warriors all together, which would mean a tribe of about 200. It was a large band for the area. Food would have to be found and brought there from many miles away.

Only Chief Medicine Basket wore his headdress, a traditional type that medicine men usually wore on official occasions. It held three feathers from an eagle's wing, an ancient scalplock and the braided intestines of a fawn freshly killed in the morning before the dew was off the grass. There were sticks of soft pine carefully carved and dyed with berry juices.

The chief sat down and motioned for Wade to sit at his right, the honored place. They

46

formed a semi-circle around the small ceremonial fire, with the sticks of the rotted pine stump laid at precise angles to invoke the spirits of the sky and the wind. The smoke drifted away from the semi-circle. Wade knew this was a good sign, and that the elders all knew it too.

Chief Medicine Basket threw a handful of powder on the fire and it blazed up with a sudden whooshing of bright flames that brought murmurs of approval from the men.

'It is time we talk. The time for worry is over. Now we talk to a man you know, you have heard about. He is Little Red Feather, and who I now name Man In Two Camps. The Roundeyes call him Wade Chisholm. He is Roundeye and he is Apache. He knows much that we do not know.'

Chief Medicine Basket gave Wade a handful of powder and indicated he should throw it on the fire. Wade looked at the powder and saw that it was pounded pitch from the pine. It was the dried turpentinelike sap and highly combustible. Wade threw it on the fire and an even bigger flame sprang up this time and consumed itself.

He frowned at the elders. 'It is a summer of tears for the Apache. Gone are the vast stretches of hunting grounds that we once roamed without seeing a Roundeye. Gone are the days when we can simply hide in the mountains and believe that the Roundeyes will let us alone, let us live our Apache lives here. And gone are the days of peace, when the Apache could move at will, and do much as he pleased. Gone are the days when our young men can raid the Roundeye ranches and villages and go unpunished.'

Several heads raised as he spoke the last.

'Gone are the old days and the old ways. The Apache is at a fork in the trail. One way leads to a new and different life where there will be problems, and worry, and hardships. But the other fork in the trail leads to war, and the Apache and all of his number have had a belly full of war. It is that simple. The old ways of the Apache, of the Jicarilla, are gone. New ways are here and more coming. Part of the new way is the Roundeye. There is no way we can survive as a people and not learn to live with the white man.

'Yes, it is true, he has smashed through our hunting grounds with his stage coaches, he has sectioned off our plains and valleys with the hated barbed wire. He has brought his women and children, built homes, forts, villages and cities. The white man is here to stay. He is as numerous as the pigeons that blacken the sky in the morning. There are more of the white men than you can count, more than the pine trees you have ever seen on the mountains. I have been to Washington, to New York. New York, it is such a large city, with so many people. You have seen a thousand Apache braves lined up on horseback ready to fight. A thousand strong extending almost as far as one brave can see. Imagine how many there would be if each of those 1,000 warriors, had a line of 1,000 warriors stretched out behind him! That is how many Roundeyes there are in the one big city of New York!

'The old ways are over. As Apache we must learn to live with the white man, to live in peace, to trust him and make him trust us. If we can't do this, the Apache nation will be blotted out, trod underfoot, scattered to the four winds, beaten into the ground like small pebbles in a muddy riverbank. All of our young men and our chiefs will be off to war, and most will never return. We will know only a valley of tears.

'The white man's ways are not all good. There are evil ones, there are vain and proud ones. Some cheat and steal and kill their own kind. But remember the Roundeye is not alone in these vices.

'The Roundeye chief has set aside four parcels of land in this Arizona land and in New Mexico to the east. He asks that all Apache come and live on these reservations, and the Apache will be allowed to live as he wishes. But he must stay on the reservation. I have not seen the land. I don't know if it is mountain or plain, desert or farm land in fertile valleys.

'I learned many things as a boy, growing up from my birth to my Chiricahua mother, Blue Feather, until I was captured by the Roundeye Pony Soldiers. One thing the great chiefs of our band taught me and all the other Chiricahua boys: that was an Apache warrior never entered a battle, or a fight, if he knew beforehand that he would lose. He did not lead five braves against five hundred Pony Soldiers. He did not charge into an enemy camp of one hundred braves, if he had only ten fighting on his side.

'We are Apache. To continue to fight the Roundeye is to go into a battle the Apache will lose. I suggest as Apaches we rely on the wisdom of our great chiefs. That we not fight, that we learn to live with the Roundeye, that we go now to the reservation.'

Chisholm looked at the chief.

Medicine Basket nodded. For a moment he stared around the semi-circle at the faces of the elders and the sub-chiefs. When he looked back at Wade there was no way to tell what he thought about the talk.

'Our people must talk. We must talk among ourselves. Man In Two Camps has the freedom of our camp, or he may go into the mountains. In four days we will be ready with our answer to you.'

Chisholm stood and looked carefully at each of the faces in front of him, including the furious countenance of Spotted Horse.

When he had made firm contact with each one he crossed his arms.

'I am Apache, I ask you to think well on what I have said. It is the only way the Apache nation can survive. I will return in four days as Chief Medicine Basket has instructed.' He turned and walked out of the council fire.

It was dusk. He knew the talk, the arguing, the shouting, the pleading would go on well into the night. Wade knew now that Spotted Horse would try to kill him. The only problem was when and where. He would be on the alert for as long as he remained in these mountains.

Four days. What would he do? He knew at once. He went back to the chief's wickiup where he thanked the chief's daughter who had prepared food for him. She was about thirteen, shy, darkly pretty, proud that she could do a woman's work for a visitor. Then he left the village, ran lightly along the faint trail downstream. He used the jogging trot that he had learned as a boy, and which he still could keep up for six hours without stopping. When he was a mile downstream, and the tiny water had grown to a main tributary of the Salt River, he stopped and searched for a place to sleep. He found a mat of soft grass near the stream, but far enough away to afford him some protection.

Spotted Horse would not come after him

tonight. He would wait until Wade returned to the camp in four days, or when he was on his way to the camp. Then Wade would be coming to him, and Spotted Horse could pick the time and place. Until then he would be comparatively safe.

He didn't bother to make a bed, simply stretched out on the last sweet grass of summer and stared up through the still leafed trees at the stars as they began to glow in the blackness beyond. He had made a good presentation, he had told them what must be told, he had showed them the way and now the rest was up to them.

Wade thought of Hannah Miller for just a moment before he went to sleep and that night he dreamed of her, the gentle girl with the open smile who had been killed so needlessly.

With the coming of dawn he was up, washed in the cold water of the stream and looked around for berries. It was late in the season but he found enough to stop his stomach from grumbling, then searched out where he would fashion his small camp. He found a spot two hundred yards from the stream up a tiny trickle of a spring flow into a stand of willow and cottonwood under the pine.

He used his knife to make a bed of leaves and moss and some tree boughs, then built a small snare with the leather thong from his waist and some stout runner blackberry vines. The snare was more of a deadfall, with the vine jerking out a prop under a small section of log he had found from an old burn. For bait he used a small piece of the jerky the chief's daughter had given him.

Wade lay concealed in the brush ten feet from the bait as he waited. He had no idea what might sniff out his bait, but he hoped it was something worthwhile, not a squirrel. He called on his early training and lay without moving for two hours, then for another half hour before he saw movement in the brush beyond.

A quivering nose pushed past a tree trunk, and then inquisitive eyes. A moment later the fox stepped warily toward the bait, its eyes darting glances from side to side, sniffing the wind, alert, curious, but wary of a trap.

The fox approached the bait and walked around it, sniffed at the burned log, then looked down at the bait. Wade had fixed it so the animal would have to reach well back under the three foot section of log to snatch out the bait. Wade held the vine in his left hand, his knife in his right.

A little further. The fox's head darted under the log for the bite. Wade jerked the vine and the log thudded down on the fox trapping it. Wade ran up, killed the fox and bled it well, then skinned it and cut up the meat and wished he had a packet of 'stinkers.'

The foul smelling matches sure would come in handy right now. He grinned, wrapped the meat in the wet skin and hung it from a branch. Then he looked around for suitable materials to make a small bow with the rawhide thong, and get together enough tinder, shavings and dry wood to build a fire with a bow and stick. Once he had a fire going, he would be sure to keep the coals lighted until he headed back for Medicine Basket's wickiup.

Wade spent three days in his little camp, saw nor heard no one, and when the fourth day came, he left with the dawn and walked toward the Jicarilla camp higher in the mountains.

CHAPTER FOUR

THE RENEGADE

Wade saw the braves coming toward him while they were half a mile off. He waited for them behind a tree and watched for some indication if they were friendly. Each man had his bow strung, an arrow in his right hand along with the bow, and two more arrows in his left hand. They moved at a trot.

Wade called to them while they were well off.

'Apaches, who do you seek?'

'You, Man In Two Camps,' they called, and all smiled and let their bows hang down as he ran up to them.

'Chief Medicine Basket asked us to come meet you,' one of the braves said. 'Spotted Horse left camp last night with four families, and he has sworn to kill you. We must move quickly.'

At the camp there was a stirring, a jumble of activity that he had not seen before. Hunters were moving into the mountains, the women were digging for roots and roasting mescal in quantities that seemed more than usual. Chief Medicine Basket sat in his wickiup, his face thoughtful. Wade sat down across from him and waited for the chief to speak.

'It is done, Man In Two Camps. We will go to the reservation. Five of my braves and Spotted Horse have chosen not to go with us. They have established a new band of Jicarillas. It could not be helped. Two more bands from the north will go with us, and we will stop by and see One Horse Thunder when we get downstream. He has told my runner that he will give us an answer by then.'

'It is good, Chief. It is good. How many in the three bands?'

The old chief nodded. 'I told them you would want to know. About 85 warriors, 85 women and 145 children.'

'I'll need to go see the General Chief in Camp Prescott.'

'Yes. We will be preparing food for the journey, and to help us live in this far away place. We will fix all the food we can. We do not have to save the doe for next year's fawns. There will be no fawns here for the Apache next year.' A tear seeped from the chief's eye and he turned away.

'I will talk with the General Chief Crook in Camp Prescott and ride back. May I borrow an Apache horse so I can make the trip faster?'

'That is the Roundye talking. A true Apache can outrun a horse any day. A horse needs too much water.' He nodded. 'Yes you may take your pick of our horses.' The old chief looked up. 'How long will we have here?'

'I'm not sure, Chief Medicine Basket. It will depend what the General Chief says about the lands, if they are ready, if they have shelters. I don't know.'

'Then go quickly and find out,' Chief Medicine Basket said. Wade nodded, said goodbye and went to find the chief's daughter. He gave her the fox skin, stretched on green willow, it would dry straight and true. She smiled as he gave it to her.

'You must dry it and tan it,' he said.

'I know what to do, I am a woman,' she

said.

He smiled, and went to the pole corral where the pride of the Jicarilla tribe pranced around. The horses sensed the new rhythm in the camp, they knew a move was coming. Wade told the braves at the horses he needed a good horse, and they selected a black for him that Wade was sure had once been an army mount.

He swung up on the broad back, took the war bridle and looped it over the horse's head, and with no formalities, rode out of the camp and down toward the headwaters of the Salt. He would not stop at the One Horse Thunder camp. Rather he would hurry on to the place where Sgt. Tim Kelly waited with his troopers.

He had ridden for almost an hour, making good time, and was past the Chiricahua camp and into the gorge of the Salt where the trail narrowed along the river and there were jumbles of fallen rocks here on both sides of the river, and the water was still so shallow you could splash across it and not even get your knees wet.

Wade rode as quickly as the trail would allow. At the place where the gorge came out into the desert, he would find Sgt. Kelly and get a new horse.

The first shot came suddenly, surprising Wade, then followed by two more and he felt the horse die under him. Wade pitched forward, spinning off the horse as it fell, twisting to miss some rocks along the trail, hitting hard on his shoulder and rolling. The rifles fired again, and he dodged behind some rocks trying to figure out where the gunmen were.

Then he knew. They were in the rocks on both sides of the trail. They had him in a cross fire, and didn't have to worry about his returning any hot lead. All he had was his knife. He drew it and tried to figure out a route along the rocks to the gunman on this side of the river. Another shot came slamming off the rock over his head and Wade surged up and lunged six feet across an open space to another rock closer to his attacker.

The gunman on the far side fired once as he ran, and Wade learned from that action that the person did not have a repeater. They were single shot rifles from the sound. He peered around the side of the rock and saw movement. He couldn't throw his knife, that would leave him with no weapon, but he could throw rocks. He gathered a dozen fist-sized rocks and lobbed them over the rocks into the position where he figured the gunman was hiding. It brought one angry yell, then a quick shot from the rifleman. Quite slowly, Wade realized his attackers were Indian, Spotted Horse he was sure now, and the brave had chosen a good spot for the attack. All that was lacking was his marksmanship for the first rounds.

Wade lay close to the ground and wormed his way around the large rock, past one barely a foot off the ground and snaked eight feet closer to the Jicarilla. The weapon across the river fired, and then Wade saw the gunman stand, and give a war cry. It was Spotted Horse. He ran a dozen yards closer, then dropped behind a rock and out of sight.

Wade smiled, remembering the lesson: when attacking, shout and yell and frighten your victims if at all possible. Spotted Horse remembered his training as well.

Wade threw another dozen rocks over the boulders protecting the second gunman, then dashed toward the rocks just as the rifle leveled over the granite. One of Wade's rocks crashed into the rifle, deflecting the shot, then Wade was directly opposite the shooter. Only the ten foot thick boulder separated them. Wade held a rock in his left hand, and his knife in his right and began edging around the boulder. It was always better to attack than wait to be attacked in hand to hand fighting.

He threw a stone to the other side of the rock, to make the hunter believe Wade was going around that side, then Wade surged around the boulder. The Jicarilla had not been fooled. He swung up the long rifle toward Wade. Wade threw the knife, dove to the ground and rolled, as he heard the blast of the rifle only a few feet from his head.

He rolled to his feet staring at the place where the gunman had been. He was down, the heavy blade extending from his belly. One hand grasped the blade as he tried to reload the rifle with his other. Wade leaped on him, grabbed the rifle and the pile of cartridges, and then eased up so he could see around the big rock.

Man In Two Camps could not see his other attacker. He fired once toward the area where he had been, but still there was no response from the other side of the stream.

There had been no horses upstream, which meant Spotted Horse had left his mounts down there. Wade rushed from one rock to another as he moved slowly downstream, trying to protect himself from the rear and the side.

Wade heard a rifle shot ahead and the scream of a horse as it went down. He ran ahead, rounded a bend in the trail, and saw Spotted Horse riding away. Wade went down on one knee, braced his elbow against his other knee and fired. The big slug ripped into the neck of the charging Indian pony and slanted upward into its brain, throwing the rider. Spotted Horse pulled the rifle with him as he fell.

Wade lay behind a rock watching the area where Spotted Horse had fallen. Now they were on equal terms. The renegade could not come back this way, he could only climb the slopes of the canyon or go down the gorge. Either way, Wade would be right behind him. He lifted, looked, then ran to the next large boulder that would offer him cover. There was no fire at him. He surged again, then again, and guessed the Indian was moving rapidly, trying to outdistance Wade, and then cut up a gully or small valley and get in back of him.

Wade stood on a ten foot high rock and looked downstream. A hundred yards ahead he saw the Indian, running, not looking back, determined to outdistance this half Roundeye.

Dropping back to the ground, Wade took up the chase, running faster than the trot, burning up the ground at a fast rate, and knowing that he was closing on his foe. But what happened if Spotted Horse found an ideal bushwhacking spot and waited for him?

Wade couldn't worry that way. He would keep his eyes open for dangerous places, and move accordingly. He knew that the man would not run away. He had come to kill an enemy, and he would do it or die trying. Wade wondered why he had brought another brave. He must have been desperate.

Here and there Wade could see the moccasin print where the running man had stepped in the softness of the sand near the water or once he splashed the water and his wet print showed for half a dozen steps.

Wade guessed they were still about five miles inside the Superstitions. There could be no help from Sgt. Kelly's unit. This was a job he had to do himself, or Spotted Horse could visit other tribes and bands of Apache in the area and try to talk them out of going to the reservation. Also, Spotted Horse would never rest until he had tried to kill his sworn enemy.

The gorge widened here where the raging winter storms sent water charging down the stream. Wade relaxed a little, but remembered that Spotted Horse still had his rifle. Many of the Indians were poor rifle shots. They knew only that you loaded it and aimed in the general direction. Still they had killed his horse.

He dog trotted now, covering the ground, changing his direction now and then to avoid making himself too good a target. The canyon narrowed again, with the sides slanting up steeply where the Salt River had bored its way through granite and basalt. For a moment below he saw a brown body slide past a boulder and vanish. The Jicarilla was still ahead of him.

Wade wondered if he could go up a valley to the ridge then run along the ridge to the next valley and come out ahead of the angry man ahead of him. He knew that he could not. He must follow and let Spotted Horse make his play.

It came where Wade expected that it might, at a bend in the gorge, where there were rocks to climb down, bad footing and all in sight of the far bank of the stream below the curve. Spotted Horse must have known that his first shot had to be good. Wade had just turned and jumped to a rock when he fired. The round touched Wade's upper arm, bored through a half inch of flesh without touching the bone and was gone.

The force of the blow spun him around and dropped Man in Two Camps between two rocks out of sight of the shooter. His right arm burned with pain. He held onto his rifle in one hand and the six rounds he had in the other. Wade looked down at the gouge in his upper arm. Painful but no real muscle damage. It would hurt like hell but he'd survive. Play dead? No, not with Spotted Horse. He was no boy playing brave. He knew all the tricks Wade did. Wade crawled six feet to another rock and peered out around it at ground level. He could see no movement at all downstream.

The Jicarilla must have been well positioned, with the rifle resting over a rock. Now what? As he watched, he saw a ledge of brown on a rock move. It was an arm. Just below it was a brown face. Spotted Horse had chosen his hiding spot well. If his arm had not moved, Wade would not have seen him.

Even though Wade could see his enemy, he could not get the rifle into position to fire without exposing himself and giving away his new spot. It would give plenty of time for Spotted Horse to pull back out of sight.

Wade concentrated on the Indian's eyes and when he saw him look away, Wade threw a good sized rock downstream into the boulders. Spotted Horse took the bait, turned staring at the spot. Then Wade whipped the rifle around. The face was gone, but the arm was still there. He fired, and saw the bullet nail the arm to the rock for a moment, then as the bullet splattered after going through the arm, the Jicarilla screamed and vanished from sight. It had been Spotted Horse's right arm, and Wade was sure it was injured worse than his own. Wade lay in the rocks watching. He had an open view of the path downstream. The Jicarilla could not move that way without opening himself to fire. Wade waited and watched. His rifle was not exposed, but in a position where he could bring it out quickly to fire.

After five minutes Wade wondered if Spotted Horse was hurt worse than he thought. No, he would not be playing dead. The brave knew that was a dying man's last trick and usually a fatal one. Only then did Wade check the rocks and the small valley opening to the left. It was possible. He stared up the tree lined canyon. Yes, probable! Staring hard, Wade began to search each area he could see. Then, a hundred yards up the slope he saw a brown form moving slowly across an open area. It was almost as if a brown rock were sliding over the land. It was Spotted Horse.

Wade brought up his rifle, aimed and fired. The round hit just above the figure and before Wade could load and aim again, Spotted Horse had rushed into some trees.

The voice came floating down with all the anger and intensity still in it. 'White man, you are not a Chiricahua. You are a Roundeye who had betrayed his adopted brothers. I will kill you and rid our tribe of you. Sleep lightly, Roundeye, I always will be after you, never forget that.'

Wade sent another round into the woods, then another. He fired the rest of his rounds as quickly as he could, then ran across the opening to the rocks below and on down the trail.

Wade trotted for a mile down the trail along the river, then bent down and washed the blood off his arm and examined the wound. It was not serious. He found some of the attatic bush, crushed some leaves and pressed them into the wound to make the bleeding stop. He held the leaves in place as he ran on. He was sure that Spotted Horse had returned to his camp. Now Wade had to get on down to the camp of the Pony Soldiers. Wade grinned. He was an Apache again. He was thinking like an Apache. That was good.

*   *   *

Sgt. Kelly sat on the edge of the Salt River with his big feet in the cool water. It had been his main amusement during the last five or six days. He had lost track. He had whittled on the soft cactus wood trying to cut free a link in a wooden chain he was trying to make. It had been one of his minor ambitions ever since he saw an old trooper doing it during the Civil War. He pressed too hard and split the top of the carefully carved link off.

'Goddamm it!' Kelly muttered.

He heard a shout from one of the troopers and when he looked up he saw Wade Chisholm standing not ten feet from him, a rifle aimed at Kelly's bulging belly.

'Bang, you're dead, Roundeye Pony Soldier,' Wade said.

'Yeah, sure as hell am. Where did you come from?'

'Along the bank in the water,' Wade said. 'It's cooler down there and anyway I thought I needed a bath before I'm company. Get the troops ready, we ride in ten minutes.'

They all rode out for Camp Prescott. Sgt. Kelly had put a shot of whiskey on Wade's wounded arm and then bandaged it for him

66

before they left. 'I think we've done some good,' was Wade's only comment to his longtime army friend. The troops and the horses were all glad for some action, even if it were only a 90 mile ride across the desert and mountains.

★　　★　　★

Two days later they arrived at Camp Prescott tired, dirty and hungry. Wade had changed back into his buckskins for the ride and now stomped into the commander's office trail weary, slapping dust off his fringed buckskins. He had no trouble getting in to see General Crook this time.

General Crook wore a pith helmet, a long white coat and white leather gloves. He had just come in from a ride on his favorite mule. He never rode a horse, claimed they were stupid and ridiculous animals. His beard had been freshly combed and stood six inches below his chin in slightly curled twin points. His eyes sparkled above his long nose and twitching mustache.

'Well? Well, Major, what in tarnation did you find out?'

'Medicine Basket is ready to come in. He wants to know what he should do and where he should go. Right now he's in the process of preparing as much winter food as he can.'

'Winter food? The government will feed

them on the reservation. Doesn't he know that?'

'He wants to be sure his people have enough to eat this first hard winter. He wants his people to have food they are used to, that will make it a lot easier.'

General Crook took off the pith helemet and handed it with the gloves to an aide, who took them and left.

'How big is this band, how many braves?'

'About 80 braves, a few over 300 in the group, including women and children.'

'Good, good. The reservation is ready for them. I've made certain there is enough beef on the hoof there so they can eat this winter. Shelter will be something else, but I'll get a dispatch off in the morning and tell them we're coming in. How long does Medicine Basket need to get everything settled?'

'I'd give him two weeks. That will dry a lot of venison jerky, and cook a lot of mescal.'

'Two weeks it is. We'll make it formal. I'll go with a detachment of a hundred men, and you of course. We'll meet the Apaches at the base of the Superstitions, there where the Salt comes out of the hills. We'll set up a ceremony and make it all official and binding. Then we'll escort the Apaches to their new home, probably in the White Mountain reservation. It is east of the Salt River canyon, around Fort Apache.'

'I'll go back and tell Medicine Basket. Two

weeks from tomorrow, on the 24th, he and his band will be there.'

'And what will you do between now and then, Wade?'

'I'll go back to the mountains, and kill deer, make jerky, and do everything I can to help my people get ready for the move.'

'Going back to the blanket?'

'Yes, if I can help my people. They are people, sir, just like you and me. When they get cut, they bleed. When they are sad, they cry. When they are happy, they laugh and sing. I know you understand that, but most of our army commanders don't. I respect you for your understanding and your compassion.'

General Crook squirmed in his seat. He never had been able to take praise, or know how to handle it. He usually turned it into a joke or pulled rank.

This time he nodded. 'Thank you, Wade, but don't let General Sheridan hear you talking that way, or he'll have me up on charges of treason.'

CHAPTER FIVE

SPOTTED HORSE WAR CRY

Wade took a rucksack of provisions when he left Camp Prescott this time. He had a ten pound sack full of beans, two loaves of unsliced bread, five pounds of hardtack that was light in color and had holes through it so it was edible, and a glass jar full of salt pork. He also had two packets of 'stinkers', the sulphur matches that smelled so badly, but which saved a powerful lot of time in lighting a fire.

Wade had two days' ride to think through what he would do. He had known that Spotted Horse would try for his hide, and now he knew the renegade brave would try again. His honor was blemished now. He had gone out with a helper to ambush an enemy whom he should have been able to kill alone, and he had failed, resulting in the death of the other brave. Such a blow to a leader's reputation could ruin any chances Spotted Horse had of holding his small group together. He might be alone now, bitter, frustrated and wandering in the mountains, his hatred growing stronger with each day.

The paymaster at Camp Prescott had insisted that Wade accept the back pay he had coming from the army for his scouting work. Wade had a habit of letting his pay accumulate at the paymasters, which meant the gold coins had to be kept in the camp safe. Now he had more than a hundred dollars in gold weighing down his pocket as he rode south. He would make a quick stop at the Phoenix Territorial Bank before he headed into the hills. There would be time to talk with Josh and Martha McCurdy at the store and maybe even to get an Irish home-cooked meal.

The horse he rode was the same one he had used on the trek to the mountains before with Sgt. Kelly. He settled into the routine of the trail, his mind open about Spotted Horse, but now he knew he would have to face the brave as an Apache, and when the contest came, one of the two would be dead.

He paused at the spot where the Salt River came into the Arizona desert. It was shallower now than when he had been there only a week ago. Usually the flow dried up completely before the winter rains came. He decided to ride into Chief One Horse Thunder's camp in his 'second skin'. It would help establish his Man in Two Camps identity for all the braves and elders. Beyond that he would watch for Spotted Horse, he would help his people gather food and help in any way he could for their move to the reservation. Wade stopped the horse and looked into the hills. Chief One

Horse Thunder had not yet told Wade if he would be going to the reservation or not. He had only assumed that the Chiricahua band would join with Chief Medicine Basket. He urged his horse quicker now along the stream bank. He would have to find out as quickly as he could.

Before he came to the turnoff toward the Chiricahua camp, Wade found the ambush spot where Spotted Horse had lain in wait for him. Wade checked and the body of the brave still lay between the rocks. Surprise etched Wade's face as he looked down at the body. Spotted Horse had not even the strength of will to return and carry his companion to a high place where his spirit would have a better chance to leave his body and float free into the heavens. Surely it could not escape the way it was. Wade vaguely understood he was thinking as any Apache would, he was not letting his Roundeye beliefs color the traditional Indian beliefs.

He drew his knife from the body and cleaned it. Restored it to his saddlebags, then picked up the body of the brave and carried him high onto a ridge, where he was exposed to the winds and the breezes and where there was no nearby tower of rock higher than the body. Now the brave was in a position where the goddess of the wind could come and help waft his soul skyward.

Wade jogged back to his horse and hurried

now, riding along the faint trail, then taking the right valley that would lead him to the camp of Chief One Horse Thunder.

Wade met a dozen women picking berries and digging roots before he came to the camp. They nodded at him and kept working. Closer to camp he saw two braves carrying in a doe slung on a pole over their shoulders. That was when he knew. Chief One Horse Thunder was preparing his people for the move. He was gathering in the second most important item to the Chiricahua, winter food.

The closer he came to camp, the more activity he found. Braves were cutting poles for travois. More deer skins were set out in the sun to dry and cure. Berries and nuts were being pounded together with dry venison and fat, mixing the whole into pemmican balls. Dozens of such balls were made and stored in a shady space.

Wade dismounted as Chief One Horse Thunder came from the wickiup. The men nodded, then Wade went back inside with the chief.

'We will go to the reservation with Chief Medicine Basket,' One Horse Thunder said. 'It has been decided. But now we prepare.'

'I have come to help,' Wade said. 'How can I help the most, by hunting?'

Chief One Horse Thunder nodded. 'As Chief Medicine Basket said, there is no need to spare the does this year, we will not be here next year to see the new fawns.'

'One warning,' the chief said. 'Spotted Horse. His band argued, fought, all but one brave has returned to our camp. Spotted Horse is alone with his woman. He has sworn to kill you, Man In Two Camps.'

'I have met him once. His shot touched my arm. He fled.'

'Spotted Horse will not give up.'

'I will be careful. As I do I will look for deer.'

'In your second skin?'

'Yes, it will help my people know that I'm truly Man In Two Camps.'

Chief One Horse Thunder approved with a slight nod and Wade went to his horse, pulled out his rifle and looked into the hills. It was afternoon. He would walk into the valley where the grass was still sweet and the deer would come to feed at dusk. Then he would return home with fresh meat for the tribe.

Wade moved well up the valley, saw two braves waiting in the brush at the side of the small stream, so he pushed higher still until the edge of the tributary was close by, and no more than a foot wide. He found what he knew was a deer trail and settled down hidden in the brush thirty yards downwind from the north, the direction he guessed the thirsty deer would approach.

The afternoon shadows lengthened, then

dusk came and with it the first tentative steps of the big deer. He had a rack with six points on each side. Wade waited until he was at the stream drinking, then he lifted the rifle and put one bullet through the beautiful animal's head. It dropped into the water.

As he had done so often in his youth, Wade hurried forward, bled the animal with a throat slash, then bound the hooves together with lengths of rawhide. He put the deer on his shoulders, holding the feet in front of him, he bound them with another thong, so the four feet were together, then with one hand on his rifle, he moved back toward the camp. Wade guessed he was about a mile away, not far. The buck weighed about 150 pounds, not a large one but enough to feed several families. Every bit of the animal would be used, that was why he did not butcher it out where he had killed it. It had been years since he had carried a deer out of the woods. Not since a hunting expedition while he was still in the army.

The United States Cavalry had been an important part of his life for so long. Since he was twelve when a friendly captain had pulled him out of a line of Indian captives and talked the colonel into letting him take charge of this one prisoner. Soon the captain had adopted Wade, christened him with a name to replace his only other one, Red Feather, and started teaching him how to survive in the Roundeye world. His flaming red hair made it obvious that he wasn't all Indian. So in the tribe growing up he had to be a little bit better at everything than the other Indian boys in order to survive. Still he was teased and baited, but he learned to live with that as well.

Then with his benefactor he learned that the Roundeyes could be just as cruel, and he suffered from his dark eyes, brownish skin, and his Indian looks. But again he took to the ways of his teachers and soon was better at most of the games and lessons than the other white boys. He had excelled in the small army post school and soon Wade was teaching the younger children. Within a year he knew more than the teacher did and came to the attention of General Will Thompson, who recognized Wade's talents and saw that he got special tutoring and instruction and then asked him if he would like to go to West Point. For years Wade had heard of the glories of the Point, and how it should be the ambition of every boy in the country. But he knew that he would never be admitted since he was half Indian.

General Thompson talked to him about it, and to his adopted parents and quietly they worked out a plan. His mother was listed as being dead, but of Italian ancestry, which would explain his dark skin and eyes. General Thompson won an appointment to West

Point from a senator in Nebraska when they were stationed there, and soon Wade was up to his black eyes in studies at the Long Gray Line home.

Wade jogged down hill along the little stream, remembering his trials and victories at West Point, and how he at last came out a second lieutenant and almost at once jumped over others to the next rank and within two years he was a captain on the general's staff. It caused dissent and slowly the rumor went around, the Captain's favorite was half Indian. He was Chiricahua! The army was a harsh master, and when half of the officers on his post stopped speaking to him, Wade knew that he soon would have to resign his commission. He loved the army, but not the army at all costs.

As he thought of those bad years, he saw movement in the brush ahead, and watched the spot, not apprehensive, but curious. He thought it might be another brave waiting for a deer. As he approached he could see it was a brave, armed with a bow, and before he could cry out an arrow lanced through the air toward him. Wade spun sideways, the heavy hindquarters of the deer covering his shoulder and he felt the arrow drive deeply into the animal. Wade dove to the ground, worming out from under the buck, and bringing his rifle to bear on the attacker. Spotted Horse was the only name he could think of.

The second arrow hit the handguard in front of the rifle, and spun away, and by then Spotted Horse had stepped from the brush holding both hands palm up in front of him.

'I have no rifle, will you shoot me down like a rabbit?'

'Yes, if I have to. You attacked me without warning, why shouldn't I shoot you?'

'Because you are half Roundeye, you will not kill me unfairly. You still have your Pony Soldier code of honor.'

'That code says the only good Indian is a dead Indian, have you heard that part of it, Spotted Horse?'

'The Roundeye gets angry, he loses his temper like a woman.'

Wade felt his anger growing. He knew the clever man in front of him wanted to make him furious, make him throw down the rifle and fight with knives. Spotted Horse held his wide bladed knife in front of him.

'Forget you're a Roundeye, fight me Apache style, man to man, blade to blade.'

'I have no wish to kill you, Spotted Horse.'

'Then I will kill you, Man of Two Evils.'

Wade stood slowly, the rifle ready. The men eyed each other and Spotted Horse laughed.

'You are not half Apache. You are all Roundeye! You are weak, you are woman! You are not fit to be called Apache!'

Spotted Horse began moving toward

Wade, his knife out and ready. Wade lifted the rifle and fired, aiming for the upper arm, and the bullet slammed home true, tearing through an inch of the Indian's arm, spinning him around, throwing him to the ground, the knife falling away.

Wade darted forward, picked up the knife and put it in his own belt, then frowned down at the renegade.

'You have killed one of your tribe already, Spotted Horse. Leave this tribe. Go and do not return. Let the tribe live in peace. You are forbidden from the Chiricahua.'

The man sat up, holding his bleeding arm. His look of hatred had intensified. Wade knew if their positions were reversed, the man would have shot him dead. Wade kicked dirt at him now, and made gestures of rejection.

'Go, unwanted, you are abandoned, you are forbidden, you are rejected by your people as unworthy of your birthright. You are no longer a Chiricahua, you are a *renegade*.'

Wade returned to his kill, lifted it to his shoulder, made sure his rifle was reloaded, then walked past the man on the ground who had not moved. His eyes followed Wade as he went by and Wade had never seen hatred more intense.

When Wade came to the spot where Spotted Horse had dropped his bow, Wade bent and picked it up and took it with him

79

down the trail. The renegade would have to find a new bow or make one before he could threaten him again. Wade hoped it would be enough to send him on his way.

The camp was smoky when Wade walked in with his deer. Two women met him and he hung the deer on pegs that had been driven into a tree. The women butchered the animal, skinning it quickly and apportioning the entrails to various families, and the heart for the chief.

Wade did not mention his second encounter with Spotted Horse. But that night he left the village and moved well to one side, lying down in an area surrounded by crisp falling leaves, that would give Wade an early warning if Spotted Horse came his way. He slept lightly, but well, and awoke the next morning ready to do what else he could to prepare the Apaches for the reservation.

That night a horse, a rifle and twenty rounds of ammunition were stolen from the Chiricahua's camp.

'It was Spotted Horse,' Chief One Horse Thunder said to Wade the next morning. Wade told the chief about their meeting the day before.

'You should have killed him,' Chief One Horse Thunder said. 'Now he will only come and try to kill you again. How many times do you think you can escape the skills of a Chiricahua brave?'

'I also am a Chiricahua—and a Roundeye. I know the best of both camps.'

'May you also have the best wisdom of both camps, as well as a sharp eye.' He paused and sighed. 'There is much to do, this is not just a move to our winter wickiups. We will make the travois for the trip. You will help us on those. No more deer. We have killed all we can dry. I will not lay waste to this proud mountain so we can stuff our bellies and let much of the meat rot.'

Wade had never made a travois, but it wasn't hard. It was simply two poles dragged by a horse, with a platform between the angled poles for the load.

Man In Two Camps did not see a sign of Spotted Horse all day.

CHAPTER SIX

SHOWDOWN AT DREAMING ROCKS

There were three more days before the Chiricahuas would start their trip to the foot of the Superstition Mountains. Three days to make the last adjustments, to get everything done, to take one last leisurely splash in the stream.

Wade was lounging in the still green grass near the chief's wickiup, talking with one of the sub-chiefs who had been most anxious to go to the reservation. He was old, and past the age when he could fight as a brave. In a few years his usefulness to the tribe would have been over if they stayed in the mountains. Now he could remain a sub-chief and sit on the council. He asked Wade question after question about the Roundeye, about their customs, their religion, their women, the children. What did they eat? What did they wear? Was it true that they were tied down to the land, that they dug in the dirt like women and planted and harvested?

Wade talked to him for an hour, then he stood. He felt the pain in his leg before he heard the crack of the rifle. The bullet grazed his left leg, passed and made a small black hole in the sub-chief's forehead. He slammed backward, the back of his head blown off, his life smashed from his body in a fraction of a second.

Wade dove to the ground and rolled away from the other people. He came up behind a rock and yelled at the others.

'Get away from me! He's aiming at me. I'm the target!' The Chiricahuas scattered. 'Bring my rifle and twenty cartridges. Put them on top of the rock near the trees. Also put my knife there.'

Chief Thunder watched him. 'You cannot go alone. We will send ten men with you.'

'No, Chief One Horse Thunder. It is my problem. You were right. If I had killed him when we met last, our friend would be alive.'

Wade turned and ran for the brush, dodging, jumping, sprinting. Three rounds came from the hidden rifle high on the hill behind them, but none touched the angry Man In Two Camps. He slid behind the rock, reached up for the rifle and the rounds, then slid the six-inch knife into his sheath and put the cartridges into his pants pockets. Slowly he took off his heavy shirt, and threw it aside, then he discarded his light brown hat. He would go after him half Chiricahua, half white man.

Wade crouched and ran for the woods. The shot that echoed down the small valley missed and Wade reached the protection of the trees and paused, thinking which way the renegade would have gone. Wade turned upward on the thrust of the slope, knowing Spotted Horse would keep to the high ground, to take the advantage of the height. Wade broke into a trot, working upward and to the left, knowing that his sworn enemy was moving in about the same direction. Neither man made a sound as he ran through the light growth higher on the slopes.

Without checking, Wade knew it was slightly before mid-day. He had eight hours or a little less of sunshine, probably about six hours. He must make good use of it. Higher.

He ran on. Once he came to a thrust of boulders and he climbed on them, lying still, staring upward and to his left. For a moment he saw nothing, then 200 yards away, along a small finger ridge, he saw the brown form, running easily, moving upward. Once over the ridge he could go down any of a dozen small valleys and there would be no way to track him.

Wade jumped off the rock and ran faster, carrying the rifle in both hands in front of him. After three or four minutes he came to the ridgeline and peered over it carefully. The horse was less than 75 yards down the slope, tied under a stubby tree. Wade rested the rifle across the brown dirt and fired. The instant the round was away, Wade rolled three times to his right and pulled back from the ridgeline. The puff of smoke from the round hung over the ridgeline like a beacon. He moved upward again, lifted up so he could see down into the canyon, then dropped down. The horse was down and probably dead. Nobody hated to kill a horse as Wade did. But Spotted Horse couldn't be allowed to use the animal. Not on this duel, it would give him victory, security. The Indian had to be in the small valley, but where? He rolled to the right and heard the shot down the ridge. The bullet hit a rock where he had been lying a second before and careened off into the air. Wade swung up his rifle, then remembered he had not reloaded immediately. By the time he reloaded, Spotted Horse had scurried over the ridge into the brush.

Wade moved down the ridge twenty feet toward the spot, then moved up to look over the ridge again, this time behind a bush. He could see no movement. Then sun glinted off shiny metal, to the left! He looked again, but the shadows closed out any more glinting. It was a direction. Wade raced along behind the top of the ridge and then slid forward. This time he caught movement, aimed and fired into the brush. There was an answering shot that came alarmingly close. Wade pulled away and came back a few seconds later, hoping Spotted Horse would guess he would make a long run.

The Indian darted into the open, jumped a log and vanished behind a rock. Wade did not fire. Where was the Indian going? There was little cover in the area to hide behind. The thicker trees were down the ravine toward the feeder stream.

Wade watched. For a moment he saw the Indian's back over the rock, then all was quiet. Wade found a rock and threw it twenty feet down the ridge on the down slope side where he hoped Spotted Horse would hear it. There was no reaction from the man below.

Wade checked through his bag of Chiricahua tricks, and all he could think of was that Spotted Horse was making himself invisible behind the rock, dusting his body with sand and soil so he could blend in, and surprise Wade when he charged through the valley in pursuit.

Wade moved cautiously along the ridgeline staying out of sight as much as possible, keeping the rock nearly in the center of the area in sight. There was no movement. He moved farther and then had the angle so he could see behind the rock.

To his surprise he saw the Indian. Spotted Horse leaned against the rock, one hand holding his leg where Wade could see blood.

'Man In Two Camps,' Spotted Horse shouted. 'I know you are there waiting. It's over. You hit my leg so I can't walk. I'm here by the rock. I'll put my rifle on top with the barrel facing my way. Come in and take me back to our camp. I'll go to the reservation. That's all that's left for me now. I'm sorry about old Eagle's Eye, I didn't mean to kill him.'

Wade watched him. He didn't rise up, he kept concealed behind the small bush, the barrel of his rifle ready but in the shade.

A half hour later Spotted Horse sat where he had been. He had not moved. There plainly was blood on his leg, but it was not gushing out. If it had been the Indian would be dead by now. Why did he say he couldn't walk? The leg wasn't broken. Wade lay there watching, his Apache patience never ending.

The voice came again.

'Man in Two Camps, come help me. My weapon is on the rock. I'll put my knife there too. I only want your help. I was wrong, isn't that enough to convince you?'

As an experienced Cavalry officer, Wade Chisholm made a decision to move in and take the prisoner; but as an Apache, Red Feather knew something was wrong. The voice, there was no pleading, no sincerity. The voice was practiced, a clever ruse. But why? What could he gain? Wade itched to have it over with here and now. How could Spotted Horse take such a chance? Wade should sight in on the renegade killer and end it quickly. But he didn't. He knew why he didn't. A true Apache would do it without thinking, without wondering about his luck. But Spotted Horse knew Wade was half Roundeye. Honor was no problem for Spotted Horse.

Wade leveled the rifle and aimed carefully. His round slammed into the receiver of the rifle laying on the rock, shattering the weapon, rendering it useless. His second shot slammed the knife off the rock into the dirt.

Spotted Horse had reacted to the first shot, but said nothing. The second shot came and he never flinched.

'Now the Roundeye believes me?' Spotted Horse asked. 'How can I harm you? Come and take me to the camp so I can treat my wound.'

Still Wade did not move. He reloaded the rifle and waited. Fifteen minutes later Wade felt his head begin to nod in the warmth.

There was a flash of movement below, and Wade saw the long immobile Indian surge up from his sitting position and throw himself over the rock. Then from the far side of the large boulder came two pistol shots. Wade ducked behind the ridgeline when he saw the weapon flash. He rolled to the left, slipped up to the top of the ridge and looked over. He frowned, then scowled. The rock from this angle had others behind it and they formed a crawl-protected outlet to the patch of thick woods thirty feet to the side of the little arroyo.

Wade checked it carefully. He could cover the exit of the rocks into the woods, but with the heavy growth there was no probability he could get a hit on the swiftly moving Apache. But to chase him now would mean losing sight of the direction Spotted Horse took once past the woods.

He waited. Spotted Horse came into the brush looking over his shoulder, ran into it and paused, then turned and went directly through the woods and over the slight rise behind him.

Wade came from his resting position on a run, angling down and across the shallow ravine and up the other side, but keeping well to the left of the other man's path.

He paused, breathing hard at the top of the rise, staring over it to the right, searching for a movement. To his surprise a rather large valley spread before him. It was a quarter of a mile wide at this point and half a mile long. They were at the dividing point on the ridge.

Wade saw the man running below. He leveled out the weapon and sighted in, leading him just enough and fired. The shot missed. Wade jerked at the weapon to chamber a new round, but it jammed. He pulled and jerked and tried with his knife, but the empty cartridge simply would not come out of the breech. Wade threw down the Springfield and ran down the slope. Now he was the one at a disadvantage. He wondered how long it would be before the hunted became the hunter. Spotted Horse vanished into a thicket near the center of the valley and Wade took a circular path, expecting at any moment to hear a pistol shot and the Apache charging at him in his now nearly unarmed state. He touched his knife, it would have to do.

Wade had circled half of the woods when he saw Spotted Horse surge out the back of it and rush for the ridge.

Wade stood in front of a boulder and called to him.

'Apache, have you lost your eyes? Why do you run away like a woman when there is a fight to be had?'

The Chiricahua turned and stared in surprise, then he hefted the pistol and walked toward Wade.

'So your Pony Soldier rifle jammed. My bow and arrow has never jammed. It is always reliable.'

'Where is it?'

'You know.'

Wade waited. The enemy was still too far away, over a hundred feet. Too far for a pistol shot, and too far for any hand to hand fighting as well.

'Does the mighty brave who shoots old men with a rifle, think he can win a fair contest between braves?' Wade asked. 'Or is he too much the woman and should tend to her roots and skin chewing.'

Spotted Horse laughed. 'Your insults are the same as when you were ten years old, Red Feather. Weak, bad, nonsense.'

'Then why does the killer of old men get angry? Why does the only Chiricahua expelled from the tribe wait in ambush to kill a brave when he could challenge him in front of the council?'

'You are not Chiricahua, you are Roundeye.'

All the time the brave came closer, the gun held at his side. He had fired twice. Wade wondered how many rounds it had in it. Often Indian pistols were found or stolen and they had only the cartridges in the chamber. There might have been five or six, or as few as two or three. Wade watched the hand with the weapon. He saw the knife near the Indian's left hand.

'You are not Chiricahua, you were expelled. You are renegade.'

'And you are dead, Roundeye!' Spotted Horse screamed the last, jumped forward and pulled the trigger.

As soon as the blued point of the pistol began to rise, Wade dove behind the boulder pulling his knife at the same time. He saw the deadly muzzle come higher and higher, saw Spotted Horse leap forward, then the sight was cut out by the rock and he hit the ground and drew back the knife.

The explosion of the pistol was loud, and at once a bullet snapped through the air just over the boulder. At the same instant the gun sounded, Wade surged upward, his arm already coming forward, aiming the knife at the last instant as he cleared the rock. His hand shot it forward. The knife drove into Spotted Horse's thigh and he dropped the gun and fell, spinning to the right, trying to pull the blade from his flesh. The gun crashed into the rock and skittered into the dirt.

Wade leaped over the rock, kicked the Indian in the side as he struggled with the blade in his thigh. Spotted Horse turned, his own knife out and slashing at Wade. Wade kicked again with the army boots he had worn this time in his Roundeye uniform and jolted the knife from Spotted Horse's hand. Wade scooped it up, then jumped to recover the pistol. For a moment he hoped it was the same caliber as his rifle and the ammunition might fit, but it wasn't. The weapon also was out of cartridges. He leveled the knife at Spotted Horse.

'Don't move, renegade, or I bury this blade in your belly.'

'Roundeye only talk,' Spotted Horse said. He whirled, Wade's blade coming from his leg, and in one swift motion he threw it at Wade. The blade bit deeply into Wade's left arm, then fell to the ground. Wade dropped the other knife, grasping his arm.

Spotted Horse was trying to stop the blood from his thigh. He limped away, watching Wade, and a moment later he was gone into the brush. Wade threw one of the knives the opposite way and ran after the Indian. It had to end here.

He found Spotted Horse sitting on a log just out of sight. Blood came from the thigh.

'Roundeye, I will not run anymore.'

Wade walked toward him warily. He may not be hurt as badly as he made out.

'Roundeye, Man In Both Camps, I must find my promontory, my pinnacle where I can sing my death song.' He held out his hand.

Wade watched him closely. 'A death song

is for a warrior, for a brave at peace with himself, and his gods.'

'I ask only a little help. There, only twice the distance of a good hatchet throw. Help me there.'

Wade hesitated, then held out his left hand, the blade still in his right. 'Careful, I'll help you.'

As Spotted Horse's hand grasped Wade's he jerked backwards, fell to the ground pulling Wade with him, his one foot coming up like a railroad drive piston, slamming into Wade's belly, driving the wind out of him. They crumpled into the dirt and rolled. Wade felt the warm blood on his legs. Fought to control the blackness that swarmed around him like a million black flies. Then he felt the tip of the knife he still held prick his chest.

His eyes jolted open. Spotted Horse had his hand around Wade's and had forced the knife to Wade's chest. Now Wade came fully conscious and he fought back the blade, twisted and pushed and forced it away from his body, back, back. Without warning the pressure on his hand vanished and the blade drove into Spotted Horse's chest. Wade pulled the knife out and stood. Blood ran from the chest cut.

Spotted Horse looked up, his eyes sluggish, lids more closed than opened.

'I don't have a death song.'

'You should,' Wade said, sitting beside him

in the sandy soil. 'Every brave makes up his death song, and changes it as he lives.'

'I lived as I believed. The Roundeyes will kill the Apaches on the reservation. They will starve our people. They will cheat us out of our lands. They will take away our hunting grounds. The Roundeyes cannot be trusted.'

'Spotted Horse, you will never have to go to the reservation.'

'I know. Now let me sing my death song, I am on my last promontory.'

Wade stood and walked a hundred yards along the ridge and sat down. He bound up his wrist with a handkerchief from his pocket, then looked back at the warrior. The death song came weakly. Wade could hear little of it. He did not want to listen. He knew when it was over and he went back to the dying brave.

'Your woman?'

'I sent her back to the tribe. Chief Thunder will let her join again and the reservation will be easier for her to live on than in the mountains. I . . . I . . . I am going to fly with the winds, soar into the sky on the wings of a giant eagle and watch the earth fall away below.'

Wade waited for him to go on, stared at the valley far down the way, then realized the Chiricahua brave had not spoken for a minute. He looked over and saw the man's eyes open, staring at the sun, his body slack, his breath forever stilled.

Man In Two Camps carried Spotted Horse to the highest point within two hundred yards and laid him on the ridge. It would do, his spirit would have plenty of room to find the giant eagle.

Wade Chisholm turned and walked back toward the Salt River. He would tell Spotted Horse's woman that he died the death of a warrior, that he would not go to the reservation and that he was in a position where his spirit could soar into the heavens. Then he would return to his work for the tribe. The time was drawing close, everything must be checked, for it would be a long march, and most of the tribe would be walking. He wondered if the Chiricahua would be allowed to keep their horses on the reservation. Wade Chisholm, the Man In Two Camps, hoped so.

CHAPTER SEVEN

POWWOW AT THE SALT

The Chiricahuas camped just outside the foot of the Superstitions where the desert takes over. They were in a small low area near the river and plainly nervous. Chisholm had talked to each of the warriors and had a stack of rifles and more than a dozen pistols carefully wrapped and bundled for the army. All firearms must be turned in before the march could start. That had been one of the pre-conditions.

A day later Chief Medicine Basket arrived with his band of more than 300 and camped across the river. The Jicarilla chief rode a white horse over the river and smoked with the Chiricahua. It was the first time such a thing had happened in memory of any brave or woman in the camp. As one of the braves had said to Wade before: 'It isn't that we can't get along with the Chiricahuas, we just don't intend to live with them.'

Wade wore his buckskins now and talked to the Jicarilla braves. The chief had instructed each of them what to do, and they filed past making a pile of the weapons they had, and Wade was impressed. At least a third of them were Springfield carbines, the issue weapon for the Cavalry. He knew there would be a lot of raised eyebrows when the weapons were loaded on a wagon.

The chiefs talked, the braves waited, the women prepared food, and the children played in the pool in the river that Sgt. Kelly's troopers had made three weeks before.

The next morning was the appointed time for the One Star General to come and talk. They would make talk, then smoke the pipe and sign the agreement. It would be official, Wade told the two chiefs. Then their people would be under the care of the United States Government, and responsible for their welfare. The Apaches would not have to go to war again.

★　　　★　　　★

General Crook was not a man to be late to an important function. He rode in at ten-thirty and brought his troops up into a formal front for an inspection, then invited the Indian chiefs to ride the inspection tour with him. The two old warriors watched in fascination as the Pony Soldiers wheeled into formations and moved around smartly to barked orders.

Wade rode at their side and when the Indians said something, Wade interpreted it for them to the Chief General One Star.

Chief Medicine Basket said something and the other chief laughed and General Crook looked quickly at Wade.

'Sir, Chief Medicine Basket said he is impressed with the fine way your Pony Soldiers obey orders and go where they are told to go. He wishes that his mounted braves had obeyed so well when he led them into battles.'

George Crook smiled. 'Tell him that I wish my Pony Soldiers were as good in the desert as his warriors.'

The comment brought smiles from the Indians and they rode back to a table that had been set up near a wagon and behind the commander's tent which had been quickly set up during the parade.

The three leaders sat in folding chairs which Chief One Horse Thunder was sure was going to fall down, but when he realized that it was solid, he sat easily and seemed to enjoy it. Wade realized it was the first chair he had ever seen, let alone sat on.

General Crook stood and faced the two Indians. He addressed them both, and with Wade translating spoke slowly and carefully.

'Great chiefs of the Apache. We are honored that you are here today, that you are volunteering to come out of the mountains of your ancestors, and move to the reservations that the United States Government has prepared for you.

'It is good that we do not make war anymore. I know the Apache have been fierce warriors, but they fight only when they have to. Now there is no more need to fight, we have agreed on what to do and as honorable men we will live up to our agreements.'

Wade had been translating as quickly as he could, and now signalled General Crook to pause for a moment. He did, and the two chiefs stirred and looked at each other.

'We will give you our guns, but we must keep our horses,' Chief Medicine Basket said.

Wade translated.

'The great Chief in Washington has decided that all those who come to the reservation willingly, have the right to keep their horses and everything else they want to bring, except firearms,' General Crook said.

'We are ready to go,' One Horse Thunder said. 'We do not need the paper, we have your word as a One Star Chief.'

General Crook decided not to go into his permanent military rank with the Indians. Neither did he want to argue with them about signing the agreement. He wanted it to send on to Washington, but he could write in the names and then show their pictograph marks. Wade would know how to do that. He moved to the small table, signed the three documents.

'Medicine Basket ready to go. We do not need the paper. Paper is easy to burn, to lose, but the solemn word of an Apache Chief will last until the tall rocks melt in the sun.'

General Crook nodded and called for a pass in review. There was nothing else to do, the ceremony itself had been far too short. He had thought of something with more showmanship. Maybe next time. The troopers came past smartly four abreast, wheeled and rode back into their parade positions.

'Are your people ready to travel?' General Crook asked.

Both chiefs said they were.

'Most of our people will be walking,' Chief Medicine Basket said. 'We hope that the pace will not be too fast.'

General Crook pondered that a moment.

'The women and children and everyone walking will lead the line of march right behind the scouts and the advance guard,' General Crook said. 'Those walking will determine the speed of the march.'

When Wade had translated, both chiefs smiled.

'You are a wise leader, an honorable One Star Chief, and a man with a heart as big as the moon,' One Horse Thunder said.

General Crook nodded, embarrassed at the praise. He turned to Wade. 'All right, son, it's up to you. Get the Apaches organized and move them out, then we'll work the troopers in where we want them. I'd suggest you put the smaller band of Indians in the lead, the Chiricahuas. You can ride near the lead if you want to or scout ahead.'

'You know where we're going, General. I'd rather walk with my people in the lead Chiricahua band.'

Admiration was shown from General Crook as he gave the word to dismiss the troops, and returned to his tent.

Wade quickly explained to the chiefs what they would do, and they listened, then swung up on their horses and rode back to their respective camps.

Within half an hour the Chiricahuas were moving. They used much the same line of march they had coming down from the mountains, a dozen or so braves on horses leading the line, followed by the women and older children. Then came the travois loaded with food, next the same rigs with the few clay pots the tribe members owned. The Apaches were not weavers, so there were no bulky looms or rugs to move. Every horse that could be ridden had a brave or an older youth on its back. The two Chiricahua cows were placed in the center of the line with six boys assigned to keep the critters somewhere near the line of march.

The Jicarillas came next with a slight separation and followed much the same order. Wade watched as a point detachment of twelve men galloped in front of the Chiricahuas. They formed a rough arrowhead with Lt. Walton in charge using his compass and heading to the east, toward the reservation.

They would swing around the base of the Superstitions and the Mescal Mountains and move toward Pinal Pass. Once over the pass, they would be in the reservation. They would proceed onward to the San Carlos agency. The whole trip would be about sixty-five miles. He would see that not a single Indian was lost along the route to sickness or accident.

Wade walked with the small ones. At first it was like a picnic, they joked and chattered, teased Wade about his red hair, and he joked back with them. Then the newness wore off and the children became quiet, as at last they realized their lives would be different from now on from anything they had ever known.

Wade watched the troopers. The general plan was for a lead scout to lay out the route, for Lt. Walton to follow that path, and for the bulk of the hundred troopers to cover the flanks riding at twenty to thirty yard intervals. A rear guard would follow with the four wagons to pick up any stragglers, any sick or injured.

General Crook rode at the head of the column for a while on his black, long-eared mule. As usual, he had on his pith helmet and long white dust coat. It was his usual trail wear and the men were used to it.

Even with their late start they made twelve miles the first day. Just before dusk, they camped at the edge of the hills on a small stream flowing down from the mountains that provided plenty of water for both humans and animals. The night soon came alive with dozens of campfires. General Crook sent for Wade and when he came, the two of them wandered through the quarter mile long camp, talking with the Indians of both bands. General Crook asked the questions and Wade translated. Many of the braves were too frightened to answer, and it usually took two or three minutes of persuasion by Wade before the men would speak. None of the women would say a word.

Wade went with the General to talk to One Horse Thunder, and they asked him to come with them on their walk. With the chief along, the people talked more freely, describing what they hoped they could do on the reservation, how they might live.

They talked well into the darkness, with the General urging the idea of farming, of planting crops and fruit trees, of growing food to live on.

'I don't see why there couldn't be some irrigation done,' General Crook said at one point. 'The land is flat enough so we could dig ditches and run the water into the fertile lands, and grow good crops.'

The Indians were cool to the idea of digging in the dirt. That was woman's work. But Crook said not in the white man's world. Many thousands of Roundeyes did nothing all day long but plant and cultivate crops and then in the fall, harvest them. He said most of these Roundeyes had mountains of wheat and corn to sell.

Later on, General Crook suggested the idea of raising cattle. Beef were good for eating as they knew, not as complete as the buffalo, but with much more meat on them than a deer. And the hide could be used in hundreds of ways as well.

Wade noted that more of the braves liked the idea of raising cattle than digging in the ground.

Back at the general's tent, he leaned back in his folding chair and twirled the twin points of his gray and black beard.

'They'll come to it, to farming and ranching. Maybe not right away, but with a little help, they will make it. I like these Apaches of yours, Wade, they are a fine and honorable people.'

The lands changed, the mountains gave way to other mountains and hills. They went through the pass and descended into the San Carlos Indian Reservation. At first it looked unbearably bleak and dry, but then they saw the hills and the streak of the San Carlos river.

It was on the seventh day that the last of the Jicarillas walked into the Agency at San Carlos. The men and the families were duly registered and the tribes set about finding a camping site where they could build wickiups that would last.

Wade said good-bye to his friends, promised that he would stop by from time to time to check on how they were doing, and how the Roundeye Indian Agent was treating them. Then Wade rode away with the Pony Soldiers back toward Camp Prescott.

On the trail they operated on the normal cavalry marching schedule:

4.45 a.m. First Call. The men rolled out of their blankets and got moving.

4.55 a.m. Reveille and Stable Call. The troops came to order, saddled the horses and harnessed the mules.

5.00 a.m. Mess Call. The troops had half an hour to prepare and eat their meal, perhaps the most relaxed spell in their entire morning routine.

5.30 a.m. General striking of camp. The busiest time of the day when the troops struck tents and stored equipment.

5:50 a.m. Boots and Saddles. The cavalrymen mounted their horses.

5:55 a.m. Fall in. The entire column assembled in line of march.

6:00 a.m. Forward March. The troop moved out.

Wade found that the trail life of a soldier was no better now than it had been before. Food which was barely passable on the camp or fort, became miserable in the field. Usually a supply wagon trailed the troop, but often its food consisted of barrels of greasy salt pork as well as the staple of dry beans, hardtack, coffee and sugar. At times the men were instructed to carry ten days worth of the salt pork and hardtack on their backs.

Wade stayed with the troops for two days, and when they swung near Phoenix, he turned off, paid his respects to General Crook.

'General, sir, I've had enough of the army for a while. I'm off to Phoenix to see about my school and what normal people do these days.'

George Crook squinted at Wade under his pith helmet.

'That offer of a major's leaves is still open, Wade. Be proud to have you in my command. You think on it some more and stop by and see me before the heavy snow sets in.'

Wade waved, snapped a salute, and rode through the Arizona desert toward Phoenix. He hit the Salt River, splashed through some of the remaining pools and then rode on to the little town. Already there were more than a thousand people in the village. He had an idea it might amount to something yet. Maybe if he were a gambler he would buy up a few square miles around the area just to see what would happen. No, not him, he wasn't a gambler, anyway, where would he get the money to pay a dollar an acre? Six hundred and forty dollars? Ridiculous. Arizona land never would be worth that much again. This was a boom time. Wait a few years, Phoenix might be a ghost town supporting nothing but smoke trees and jackrabbits.

He shrugged and continued through the east side of town where he saw two new houses going up, and moved on to Main Street. They were even talking about giving the street a new name. Wade tied up in front of the McCurdy General store and stomped inside.

Josh McCurdy was wrapping up some crackers and prunes for a customer.

'Where the hell are the wild women, the whiskey and the poker games in this town?' Wade yelled at the top of his voice.

Josh McCurdy jumped in surprise, then swore softly and grinned.

'I'll be damned, the bad penny, it's back again.'

CHAPTER EIGHT

POLECAT ON YOUR HINDSIDE

'Wade Chisholm, we got ourselves one bucket full of trouble,' Josh said as soon as the customer had gone.

'Trouble? I just herded over 500 Apaches into a reservation, cleaned out the west side of the Superstition Mountains of Indians, and *you* say we got trouble? We just lost our trouble.'

'Not that kind of trouble. You remember that shyster, half-assed lawyer kid who helped us set up the trust fund and everything for the school and the foundation or whatever it is?'

'Sure, young guy by the name of J. Lawson Ambrose. He set up the papers for us.'

'He also set up something else for us. He's found an heir to the Hannah Miller estate. I got papers this morning. His client is suing us. He claims that he is a first cousin and had stayed with the Millers on and off for a couple of years. He's demanding the territorial district court that he be named the legal heir of the entire estate, and that our foundation be prevented from spending any more of the estate's money until the situation is resolved by the court.'

'Ambrose did that to us, even after we paid him that three hundred dollars in legal fees?'

'He sure as hell did.' Josh pulled out his fifth of whiskey and poured two shot glasses, handed one to Wade. 'And the word I hear is that this so-called cousin has offered to give Ambrose half of everything he gets out of the court case.'

'Half. Well. Ambrose is shooting high. He could come out with fifteen, eighteen thousand dollars.' Wade lifted the shot glass and downed the whiskey, wincing and shaking his head for a minute. 'What did you refill that bottle with, Josh, turpentine?' He sucked air into his mouth for a moment. 'Lordy that is the worst whiskey I've ever tasted.'

'Whole thing leaves a bad taste in my

mouth too. Has this skinflint Ambrose got a case against us? Can he do this?'

Wade nodded. 'Oh, he can do it, he can file charges. All we have to do is be ready to prove that what we did was just and right and within the law, and will benefit the community as we said it would in our charter. Now all we need is a lawyer who is smarter than Ambrose. And it shouldn't be a hell of a hard job to find one.'

The friends looked at each other, then Wade poured another shot for both of them, and they drank the shots down in one gulp and went back toward the front of the store.

'I'll get a bath, a room, maybe a new shirt and go lawyer looking. Any new ones in town since I was here last?'

Josh shook his head.

'Then we do some scratching. How is that man Ralph Kleen coming along with the finished drawings?'

'He's almost done. He wants to start moving dirt, getting in some foundations.'

'Hold on, we don't even have the land yet.'

'Almost. Kleen and I found a spot just on the edge of town. It's only five acres but we figured it would do for a start.'

'It's on the river?'

'Close enough we figure, we'll go look at it anytime you're ready.'

'First we better get this lawyer situation cleared up.' Wade frowned. 'I better get moving, I can't do anything looking like I just came out of the bush.'

'You got your Indians moved?'

'Safe and sound. Now if Uncle Sam just treats them right, things around here should settle down, maybe for good.'

*   *   *

Two hours later Wade had a new set of clothes on, black pants, white shirt and string tie, a red checkered vest and a jacket that almost matched the pants. He felt like a dude, but it felt good to be dressed up again. It reminded him of weekends from the Point when they used to go into town that last year. He found the building he was hunting, just past the livery stable and two doors up from the bank.

Handsome Jones had struggled with his name ever since his doting mother saddled him with it, and by now had heard every possible joke that could be built around the name and the situation. While others were thinking up old jokes, he was evaluating the persons he talked to and figuring out their flaws, soft spots and problems. The practice had kept him in food and shelter for twenty years and kept him moving west at the same time. He had decided this was as far as he would travel, he wanted to settle down here and had visions of making the desert flower.

All they needed was water.

Handsome Jones looked up as the stranger with the red hair walked in.

'Mr. Jones, seems that you're a lawyer. You looking for a client?'

'If I can help you sir, I'd be pleased. As you see, my office and my calendar are both uncrowded.'

Wade grinned and sat in a chair next to his desk. Briefly Wade spelled out the problem, and the middle aged man wrote quickly on a pad of yellow paper. When Wade finished, the lawyer looked up smiling.

'This Ambrose, I haven't met him, but he's young, right? And trying to make it all in one swing. That isn't uncommon in the East, to take on a problem and split the profits between the litigant and the attorney. It's frowned on by reputable lawyers, and it would be my hope that this factor might be in our favor with the circuit judge. I understand Judge Maxwell may be around in two weeks. Do you have the papers they gave to you?'

Wade pulled out the envelope he got from Josh and gave it to Handsome Jones. He read the three pages quickly and looked up smiling.

'This is mostly doubletalk. This Ambrose has a way with words but he's short on facts, on the law, and on just about everything else. The only one who can stop you from spending any of the money in the trust is the judge with a court order or an injunction. That can't be done until the judge gets into town. He'll sit here in Phoenix for about two weeks. We should be able to get it all cleared up in that time. Oh, I'll want to see the papers that Ambrose drew up for the formation of the non-profit group and the trust fund.'

'Then you don't think there's any problem?'

'Problem? Of course there's a problem, Mr. Chisholm. I take it you are Wade Chisholm?' Wade nodded. 'The problem is exactly how you came to be in possession of the funds in the first place, and how you took it upon yourself to channel these funds into a charitable endeavor. Was there a search made for relatives? How extensive was that search? What were the results? Then how well can this "cousin" establish his claim to the estate? It may take some doings, but most judges I've known would side with the charitable function. I'll begin at once to do a background search on the cousin. It should be our hope that he's a fiddle-foot, a roamer who has been in his share of jails in the territory, who has a record on file with the marshal here, and who only stayed with the Millers because he was destitute and they took pity on him. However if he is a cousin, that would mean son of a sister or brother of one of the adult Millers, it might open up other relatives. We'll have to search it out.'

'And just what would your fee be for such a job, Mr. Jones?'

'Fee? I never said anything about a fee. Just my expenses in the search, which should be minimal. If we win the case and you keep the school, I'd like to represent you. If we lose and there is no school, then I'll apply to the judge for legal fees from the estate since it is a charitable institution that is being lost. So it shouldn't cost a lot. I want to build a reputation in this territory, and fighting a good fight on the right side never hurt any lawyer.'

Wade liked Handsome Jones. 'That is kind of you, sir. I'll get the rest of our papers from Josh McCurdy and bring them here right away. Oh, I hope you don't mind a personal question. Could I give the papers to you over a thick steak over at the Phoenix Hotel? Not the fanciest in town but the steaks are good.'

Handsome Jones smiled. 'It would be a pleasure. I hate eating alone. Shall we say about seven? I usually take a late meal in the evening.'

Wade walked back along the dusty street, dodged a buggy and stepped up to the boardwalk in front of the general store. Inside he found Josh who had brought Martha in to mind the store so he could take Wade out to the proposed site for the school.

Both men rode, Josh getting a

pinto-spotted pony from in back of the store. Wade was surprised how close it was. The area led back toward the river from a street that had the unlikely name of Van Buren. There were no houses out that far, and Wade guessed they had come less than a half mile from the store. The land was fairly level, with a few clumps of grass and cactus, but no large growth. It was the usual Phoenix topsoil, ten parts of sand to one part of rocks and pebbles. The back of the area stretched out toward the river which was about four hundred yards away.

They rode the thousand foot long boundary, then turned to where a stake with a red ribbon hung. It was the side of the 200 foot wide lot. Just over five acres.

'How much they want for it?' Wade asked.

'They started at $200, but I got them talked down to $150. This Monroe claims it's city type land and should be higher priced. He's heard about the school, knows we have the money, and is trying to hold us up.'

'Does he own the land on both sides of this lot?'

Josh said he thought he did.

'Then go back to him and tell him we'll take it, but only if he sells us three pieces this size. We want fifteen acres, the other two toward town from the first one. And offer him $400 for the 15 acres. Tell him he has five minutes to decide, and that the deal must

114

be finished, closed, and registered in the courthouse by tomorrow noon. If he doesn't take the deal we can get property in ten other places. Oh, put the sale through the trust fund's new lawyer, Handsome Jones.'

Josh grinned. 'You really believe in getting things done, don't you, Wade? I'd bet that old Monroe will snap up the deal. He picked up the square mile in that spot ten years ago for a couple of steers way I hear it.'

That night at their late dinner, Wade and Handsome Jones got to know each other better. Jones was surprised when Wade said he had graduated from West Point and had been in the army for four years.

'Yes, the Point, a fine institution, and a good education. That's what's so important today, a good education in the basics. I spent some time at Harvard in Boston, then finished my legal studies in Princeton.'

'Yes, in New Jersey,' Wade said. 'I did some research work there on a project I was doing at the Point.'

'How interesting.' He turned back to the problem. 'I've done some inquiring about our friend Marvin Clobes. He isn't a hard man to find. He's about thirty, single, has been a cowboy, soldier, spent some time in Texas, came to this area about a year ago, and did in fact live with the Millers at one time for almost a month. He has been in the local lock-up twice, both times the marshal says for drunk and disorderly. Not the kind of good solid felony charges I had hoped for, but better than nothing.'

'What does he look like?' Wade asked. 'Is he in town right now? Maybe I should have a talk with him, convince him that he's just wasting his time.'

'Wrong, Wade. Bad idea. That's the direct approach and it won't work in this case. Time means nothing to Clobes, and he isn't spending a cent of his ill-gotten cash. Ambrose is taking it on strictly for the percentage. If he doesn't win the case, it doesn't cost Clobes a cent. He'd be a fool to turn down something like this. He has everything to gain, and at absolutely no risk.'

'So what do we do?'

'You do nothing. Go about your normal business, and let me handle the legal matters, including the research. If I find there's something to be found in an outlying area, I'll see if you want to ride there to ask some questions.'

He paused and chewed on the forkful of deliciously rare steak. 'You're right, they do cook up a good steak dinner here. I thank you for the suggestion.'

Wade told him about the land purchase.

'Yes, good idea, get it done, finished before the courts can get involved. Then you have your start. I would suggest you begin construction as quickly as you can. Yes, yes, that will impress the judge that this trust fund isn't some kind of a sham or a shield so you can use the money yourselves later on.' He chewed on some of the mashed potato smothered in sour cream, chives and tinged with black pepper and salt. 'Yes, your board of directors, good idea, but make it larger. This is an unpaid honor to be on this board. Have at least 30 names. Get the best people in town, and have at least two or three preachers, the publisher of the little newspaper I saw, merchants, any society folks there might be, and the two or three richest men in town. That's your next job. With 30 of the town's leading citizens on your board of directors, the judge will almost certainly believe that this is a legitimate charity operation.'

Jones paused and stared directly at Wade. 'Mr. Chisholm. This Hannah Miller Children's School is legitimate, isn't it? It is exactly as you have explained it to me?'

'Yes, Mr. Jones, it is. It's named after a woman I wanted to marry, and never had the chance before some drifting outlaws killed her. I want this school more than anything I've ever wanted in my life.'

'Good, I believe you. Now we need concrete actions. I'd like to see some foundations in, some adobe curing, and detailed architectural plans before we go into court.'

'You'll have it, Mr. Jones.'

'Oh, one other question. You are dark, and your black good looks and black eyes . . . are you part Indian?'

'Yes, Chiricahua. My mother was Blue Feather, a full blooded Chiricahua, and my father a red-headed Irishman.'

'Striking.' He smiled. 'I bet somebody had to pull some strings to get you into West Point, knowing the army's feeling about Indians. I'm sorry if that's out of line.'

'Not at all, Mr. Jones. I'm as used to that as you probably are to jokes about your name. I do have one question. You seem qualified to practice law. Is there any tests to pass in this territory to allow you to practice?'

Jones chuckled. 'I wondered when you would ask. No, absolutely no requirements or tests or boards to pass. No bar to pass as there is in the East. It will come. Now anyone who wants to can hang out a sign and proclaim himself a lawyer. I'll be glad to show you my degree when we get back to my office.'

Wade shook his head. 'Not necessary, what I've heard so far, I like, and I agree with your approach.'

A man bumped into the table, upsetting a water glass. He was short and heavy, had eyes that had seen the bottom of too many empty glasses for too long. He wore range clothes and a grimy leather vest over a plaid shirt and still wore spurs and his dusty hat.

118

'Which one of you gents is Wade Chisholm,' the man said, his speech slurred just enough to reveal the Dutch courage showing through.

Both men at the table stood.

'Allow me,' Jones said. 'Mr. Wade Chisholm, this is a man well known in Phoenix, Mr. Marvin Clobes.'

CHAPTER NINE

THE SET UP

Wade stared at the smaller man, curious just what kind of a man Marvin Clobes was, anxious to find out. First appearances did not make a good impression on Wade. Clobes had drunk far too much and probably too quickly, and evidently had come searching out Wade Chisholm. He carried a six-gun tied low on his hip where it was closer to his hand for a faster draw.

'You were looking for me, Clobes?' Wade asked.

''Peers as how I was. You the one what knew my kin, Hannah Miller?'

'That's right.'

'You the one what's trying to steal my inher . . . all of that money that's s'posed to come to me?'

'Now who told you anything like that?'

'Ambrose did. Yes sir, he sure did. He told me that there was just a pile of cash money involved, and that it should have been mine, and he'd help me get it.'

'So of course you said fine and dandy,' Wade said.

Clobes belched, but didn't seem to notice. 'Well, hell, sure. Me, I never had no money. And them distant relations of mine didn't look like they ever had any either.'

'Mr. Ambrose contacted you first then, Clobes?' Jones asked.

'Huh? Oh, damn right. He said he had wind of a good deal and since I'd stayed at the Miller place for a while, maybe I could get some of the money.'

'Mr. Ambrose would take the rest?' Jones probed.

'Well, like he said, he deserved something for finding me and telling me and all. I guess he deserves some, don't you think he does?'

'Which side of the Miller family you on? You Mr. Miller's brother's boy?'

'Yeah, yeah, that's right. Paw and Miller were brothers. Yeah, right.'

'Then how come you have different last names?' Wade asked.

'Oh, well, hell I don't know. Just do.'

'Were you sweet on Hannah Miller, Mr. Clobes?' Wade asked.

'Hell, sweet on her? She was so uppity she

wouldn't give a mule the time of day. Tried to get her in the barn once, but hell, she was all prissy and pure. Couldn't even touch her tits.' He leaned closer. 'Think she was one of them queer kind, you know a girl who likes to get all lovey with another woman.'

'So you want to get even with her?' Jones asked.

Clobes blinked and looked at Jones. 'Who the hell are you?'

'I'm Mr. Jones, attorney for Mr. Chisholm in the suit you initiated through Mr. Ambrose.'

'Yeah, you talk like a lawyer feller.' He turned and faced Wade. 'You the one I want to jaw with. You just give me five thousand dollars and I'll ride out of town and you'll never see me no more.'

Wade started to respond but Jones touched his shoulder.

'I'm afraid we can't do that, Mr. Clobes. You're going to get exactly nothing out of this subterfuge, not one thin dime, and then you're going to be ridden out of town on a rail with a little tar and feathers on you.'

'Okay, okay,' Clobes said. He stopped, blinked three times, and then seemed to steady. 'Hail, I'll make it two thousand and I'll leave tonight.'

'Not one copper cent,' Jones said. 'Now if you'll excuse me we must be going.'

What happened next came so quickly,

Wade wasn't sure he had it all sorted out exactly right. Clobes pushed Jones, shoving him back against the table which tipped over in a crash of dishes, glasses and silverware. A half dozen patrons in the dining room gasped and looked at the three men.

Wade responded, shoving Clobes to one side, where he tipped over an unoccupied table and his hand dug for his gun. Wade's booted foot slammed upward hitting Clobe's hand just as it touched the gun smashing it away from the iron. Wade followed through with a round house right fist into Clobe's jaw that sent him dropping on the overturned table. His six-gun had dropped to the floor and hadn't fired. Wade picked it up and handed it to Jones, and they both turned and left the dining room.

At the desk Wade told the clerk to put the damage on his bill and then they went outside, walked down half a block and stepped into a dark alley and watched the hotel front door.

Clobes came out suddenly, propelled by two men. He lost his footing and fell in the street, mashing a half dozen horse droppings as he went down. He staggered to his feet, tried to brush himself off, then weaved down the street heading for the nearest saloon.

Jones leaned against the wall of the building and lit a long, thin cigar.

'We may have bit more of a problem now

than we did before. Ambrose will make a lot out of that little scuffle. Try to show that there is an anger between you and his client, that you set up this whole school idea just to deprive Clobes of his rightful inheritance.'

'Probably, but I've got a better lawyer who will set things right.'

'Don't count on it, Wade. Just because we're in the right is no sign that we'll win. Justice is blind, she really doesn't care who is right, as long as it's just. And by "just" is meant who has made the most convincing argument. This could get sticky. What's involved, about thirty thousand dollars? That's more money than most men make in a lifetime.'

'If I was a gambling man I'd say that this Clobes is no more kin to the Millers than you are, Mr. Jones. And I want you to prove it. Couldn't we do that by finding out exactly who his parents are? If neither of his parents are related to the Millers than he damn well can't be.'

'Correct, young man, and I assure you finding his parents is high on my fact finding list. But ancestors can be a tough track to discover in the West, as you must know. We'll do what we can. I hope to have enough ammunition ready to answer the charge just as soon as it is accepted by the court. Now, I better be getting back to my office. I have some work to do.'

'Right. I'm at the Phoenix hotel if you need me. I'm on the third floor, 312, the corner room in front.'

They parted. Wade talked to Josh first.

'Tarnation, Wade. You expect me to know everybody in town. Place is getting too dab-blamed big for that. When we had two stores and ten houses I could name them—kith, kin and strangers. Now I'm happy if I know half the folks in town. You know we had four new houses start last week! Place is growing like the mumps.'

'Think back. The Millers only came 'two years ago, you said you remembered that. He came in for some supplies when he put up his new house.'

'Sure, but we didn't talk about any kin he might or might not have. And you remember when we went through those charred letters and papers from the house. We found addresses in the East but none of them were for relatives. No parents, no uncles or aunt, only friends. I think it's a dead end.'

'So we have to prove who Clobes is and who his parents are.'

'Easier. I hear he came here from Prescott or Flagstaff. Now that ain't too far away.'

'Wish we had a telegraph through here, sure would make life a lot easier.'

'So you can ride up there and see what you can see. By the time you get back we'll have the foundations dug for the first building. We put up the dormitories first, right? So the kids would have a place to live. At least that's the first one we'll start on. Past my bedtime. You be quiet now so I can get some shuteye and turn out the light when you leave.'

Wade laughed, slapped Josh on the shoulder and hiked back to the hotel. He could use a good night's sleep himself, now that he knew what he was going to do the next day. He would play detective and see what he could do about tracking down Clobes' kin.

Wade walked past two saloons and was tempted to try his hand at the faro tables, but didn't. He would have time for some relaxing after this was all over.

At the desk of the Phoenix Hotel he found out that the ruckus in the dining room had cost him three dollars and fifteen cents, all for dishes. He paid it and went up to his room on the third floor. He lit the kerosene lamp and lay on the bed thinking through what the day had brought. Another surprise, another problem standing in the way of the Hannah Miller School. They were on the right track now with the lawyer Jones. He was good, and was interested in doing a good job to build his reputation. Wade felt that they would win in the court, but with a man like Marvin Clobes involved you never could tell what might happen. Clobes was the type who seemed to enjoy direct action. Like his coming up to them at the table in the dining room, even though he was half drunk.

Wade took off his new shirt and new pants and slid under the quilts. He could count on his fingers the number of nights he had spent under a roof in the past three months. It was an unexpected pleasure. He rolled over and the gouge in his arm from the bullet pained him so he rolled back. The lamp had been blown out ten minutes ago, but still he lay awake. He didn't expect any visitors, that was one reason he picked a corner, third floor room. Nothing but a fly or a squirrel could crawl up to his window, and the door was locked with a straight backed chair slanted under the door knob.

Soon he slept.

Wade woke some time later, but he couldn't tell what time it was. He had heard something, was it in the hall or in his room? The sound came again and he realized the sound was from the roof. Someone was above him. He hadn't expected any danger from the roof. He got up quickly, quietly and pulled on his trail jeans and wool shirt. He had just reached for his gunbelt which hung on the bedpost when something crashed through the side window and fell on the bed. It was a man who had been on the end of a rope, and when he crashed through the glass he carried the thin curtains on his feet and now lay on the bed in a tangle of muslin and boots.

But before Wade could reach his six-gun the man yelled at him.

'Hold it right there redhead! Move another inch and I'll blow a .44 sized hole right through your worthless gizzard.' The gun barrel glinted in the moonlight streaming through the naked window, and Wade could see enough to know the gun was pointed his way. Wade held his position, watching for a hint of who his attacker was. He knew it had to be Clobes, but the voice didn't sound right.

The man on the bed lifted the gun and pawed at the curtains, tore them free and stood beside the bed. Now Wade could see that it was Marvin Clobes.

'Clobes, what the hell you doing, breaking into my room? I'm going to have you arrested for robbery. That will put you away for five years at the territorial prison at Yuma.'

'Shut up, injun, I just heard tell about you. Squaw for a mother and a no-good gold digger for a paw. No wonder you turned out a no-good.'

'You come here to shoot me or talk me to death, greenhorn?' Wade asked.

'Oh to shoot you, cause then I'd get the thirty thousand dollars and wouldn't have to work no more at all.'

'Who told you that, Ambrose?'

'You just don't never mind that, injun.' He raised the gun now to center on Wade's chest.

'You gonna be a good injun in a minute, so it don't matter none. That lawyer fella of yours shore has scared that lawyer of mine. Says he's a good one, and it'll be hell-hard to beat him in the court.'

'So you're trying it another way. You'll just take what you want,' Wade filled it in.

Wade had been thinking, grabbing at any faint ideas for help. His gun was too far away. Clobes stood beside the bed but nearest to the door. There was no scatter rug to pull out from under his feet. Nothing to grab and throw. Not even an over-stuffed couch to dive behind. Nothing.

'Look what you did to the window,' Wade said.

Automatically Clobes glanced that way as Wade hoped he would and Wade dove straight at him, got under the roar of the pistol aimed over his head and hit Clobes with all his weight just above the knees. They drove backward. Another round went off in the ceiling and then they were down, rolling, kicking, the gun clattered under the bed. Wade rolled Clobes the other way.

If it had been half light Wade would have seen it coming and ducked, but the boot came slamming at his head, glanced off his forehead and dropped Wade to the floor, groggy, unsure, of what was going on. There were footsteps now in the hall. Someone rattled the doorknob.

128

'Hey, what's going on in there?' a muffled voice shouted through the door.

Wade surged to a sitting position. Clobes started for the door, Wade's six-gun was behind him on the bedpost. Wade stood up. Clobes rushed to the window, grabbed the rope and stepped out onto the third floor window frame and then he was gone.

Wade staggered to the door, kicked the chair away and unlocked the door. Two men ran in with lighted lamps. One of them had a gun.

'Out the window,' Wade gasped, and the man with the gun ran to the opening and looked down.

'Some fool on a rope,' he said.

'Shoot him!' his partner urged.

'Too late. He's got a horse down there and he's heading out of town like a shot.'

The attention turned to Wade. They sat him down, put some alcohol on his forehead over the boot scrape, then cleaned the glass off the bed.

Dr. Anderson, a widower, and the second doctor in town, lived on the second floor, and he was roused out of bed to come tend to Wade. He said it was nothing to worry about, dabbed the alcohol on again and told him to get a good night's sleep.

The night clerk rushed up with a blanket and tacked it over the broken window, and kept muttering that somebody was going to have to pay for the new window, and Wade knew it would show up on his bill.

It was almost an hour before everything was cleaned up, the people left his room, and Wade could get back to bed. He slept little until it was daylight, then got up, checked his gear and packed the new shirt and pants in a small valise he had bought the day before, and went downstairs and checked out. The broken window cost him three dollars.

'We have to get them shipped in by stage or freighter all the way from St. Louis,' the clerk said. 'At least half of them get broken on the way, that's why they cost so much.'

Wade hadn't asked, and as he looked over at the dining room, the clerk said it would be open at seven, over an hour away. Wade took the change from his twenty dollar gold piece, walked to the livery stable and ransomed out his army mount, saddled it and rode to Josh McCurdy's place. He was eating breakfast and welcomed Wade in for a bite.

Three eggs and two stacks of flapjacks later, Wade told the McCurdys what had happened the night before.

'Damned fool,' Josh kept muttering. 'He must have been drunk again, maybe still drunk. Jones told me they had a good chance of getting half of the estate if Clobes could come anywhere near proving that he was a distant relative. Now he probably blew his chances on even that.'

'I hope so. I'm on my way to Prescott and then Flag if I have to. I want to come back with some affidavits swearing that his family is no relation to the Millers.'

Before he knew what she was doing, Martha McCurdy had packed him a lunch.

'Now, never you mind, Wade Chisholm. Least I can do for any man who's going to ride all the way to Prescott. Mercy, I went up there once three or four years ago on the stage. Mercy, I thought we never would get there. And then it was so cold I near came to freezing my ears off.'

Wade thanked her, gave her a kiss on the cheek and watched her blush and hurry into the kitchen. Josh chuckled and led Wade out to his mount.

'You got any spare cartridges?' Josh asked. 'Hate to see a man go out on a two day ride short on firepower.'

They went to the store and Wade picked up a box of twenty-five 44 caliber rounds and a box of 20 rounds for his Springfield carbine. He liked a repeater but they were too long for a saddle scabbard.

Wade grabbed a handful of prunes from the barrel, waved at Josh and went out the back door. A moment later he was off and riding for Prescott.

CHAPTER TEN

SURPRISE IN THE TIMBER

Wade figured he'd take his normal two days to ride into Prescott. He could bunk at the army camp for a couple of days while he turned the town inside out for any more people named Clobes. He hoped that he could get his paper signed by Clobes' kin and be back on the trail a day or two later. That was the way he planned it.

Wade came out of the first good grove of timber along the trail and ahead saw a glint of sun off metal. He lunged to the side of his horse away from the glint and almost at the same time a rifle barked ahead of him and the bullet parted the air two feet over the saddle. He swung the horse into more trees until he was shielded from the trail.

The tall redhead didn't even stop to think who had tried to bushwack him. He knew. It had to be Clobes, and he was trying to stop him from getting to Prescott. Somehow he heard or figured out what their strategy was going to be. Or perhaps Ambrose, his shady lawyer, had figured it out as well.

Wade swung down from his horse and moved through the timber on a run, his Spencer in his hands, cocked and ready to

132

fire. He came on the slight turn in the trail cautiously from heavy brush in the mountain chill. The rider was not there. He could see where the horse had been tied, where the gunman had waited behind a rock, and dug his boot toes into the ground as he hunkered down waiting.

Wade ran back down the stagecoach road to his horse and moved out again, keeping closer watch this time. But there was no more trouble. Either the bushwhacker thought he had been identified, or had given up. If it was Clobes, Wade knew he hadn't given up. He was after the biggest haul of his life.

After a talk with the post office in Prescott, Wade had a list of three Clobes families. They said they weren't supposed to give out addresses, but the clerk knew where two of them lived and he drew a rough map. One was in town, the other on a spread five miles into the hills.

Wade checked the closest one first. It was a clapboard house, with a small picket fence around it, and the whole thing painted white, with some late roses still blooming by the door. The man who answered the door was in his seventies, white hair and a problem with his hearing. He waved Wade inside without understanding a word, and his frail, bird-like wife stepped up and patted his arm.

'Good morning, young man. I'm Mrs. Ira Clobes, what can we do for you?'

'Morning, Ma'am. My name is Wade Chisholm and I've got a few questions. Trying to locate a man by the name of Marvin Clobes. Would he be any kin of yours?'

'Marvin Clobes,' the woman repeated. 'No, not that I can think of. My sister had a Marvin but her last name was Winters, and that's back in Winchester.'

The old man looked at the door across the room that was open an inch, and Wade wondered why. Then he figured it and stepped toward the wall so he would be out of the range of any sudden lead from the door.

'No, young man, I don't reckon we have any kin out here by the name of Marvin. Sorry we couldn't help you none. But that's just the way it is. There's another Clobes out by Pilot Knob, but they ain't kin to us. Maybe they the folks you hunting.'

The old man grinned and nodded. 'Marvin, shore as hell a no good. You said Marvin, Milly?'

'We don't know any Marvin, Ira, now hush up.'

'Hail, we know Marvin. He's Willy's boy. Been here to dinner just last night. What the hail you mean, woman?'

The shot came from the half open door, and Wade had drawn his six-gun and held it by his leg waiting. As the shot thundered in the small room Wade blasted twice into the small opening, then rushed up and kicked the door open staying well back of the wall. Another shot came through the open door, smashing a china plate hung on the opposite wall.

Wade heard a door slam as the sound of the shot faded in the room. Then he heard a cry of anguish.

Behind him Ira Clobes lay on the floor, a growing crimson splotch on his chest. He tried to hold his head up, but couldn't. Wade rushed to him, saw that the bullet had missed his heart but splattered through his left lung. The blood seeped through his fingers as the old man moaned. He coughed and spit up blood.

For a moment a froth of bloody bubbles appeared below his nostrils, then he wheezed once more, formed some silent words with his lips and his head rolled to one side. Ira Clobes was dead.

His wife leaned down on his long, thin body and began to sob.

Wade rushed out the front door, around the house and studied the ground. It wasn't so dry that he couldn't follow the tracks of a frightened man running. He angled across the back of the yard, into a street, crossed it and went between two houses. Wade ran after him, low and angry. Now Clobes had more to answer to than just being a no-good. He had killed that old man, a relative, one of his own tribe. Wade had reloaded the six-gun as he ran. Now he darted from one side of the houses to the other as he moved ahead. He found the end of the trail in an alley, where a horse had left in a rush just moments before. Wade dog trotted after the prints until he saw the direction they took, then he ran for his own horse, leaped on and got back on the trail.

It was not more than ten in the morning when Wade followed the trail out of Prescott toward Flagstaff. At first it seemed like the man on the run wasn't trying to hide his tracks at all. Then he cut through a small stream and didn't come out on the other side. It took Wade a half hour working both banks before he found the trail again.

Wade took a chance, figuring Clobes would play a half dozen trail dodging tricks before he was through. Wade got back on the Flagstaff trail and rode hard for half an hour, then let his horse rest for fifteen minutes at a slow walk, then rode hard for another half hour. By that time he was sure he would be ahead of Clobes.

He tied his horse to a tree off the trail, found a good position behind a rock and a small pine tree and settled down to wait. The sun overhead bored down with a welcome warmth as he waited. Wade watched a small beetle crawling along the dirt of the forest floor, struggling over dropped pine needles, working around rocks, but always moving toward the west. He wondered where the creature was going. For a moment he thought how useless the small thing was, what good did it do in the world? Then he remembered something about the food chain in the forest, how even the smallest bug had smaller ones that it fed on, and in turn was fed upon by larger creatures.

He tried to see the beetle again but it had vanished. As he searched for it he heard hoofbeats down the road. Clobes had finished his tracking games and was riding in earnest for Flagstaff.

Wade had picked an ambush point where he had the advantages. The wheels of the stage coaches had cut a narrow gully here between the boulders and trees making it hard to ride out of the trail. The land sloped up on both sides which again would slow down a rider. Wade had no plans of killing Clobes, not even wounding him from ambush, but he did want to stop him, capture him and take him back to Prescott for trial. The marshal there would probably be forming a posse to ride after him.

Wade waited as the rider came closer. He picked the spot he would fire his six-gun in front of the horse. That would be enough to bring it to a halt, he hoped. Wade waited, then at the exact time fired in front of the horse.

Marvin Clobes jerked on the reins, then

started to spur ahead.

'Hold it, Clobes or you're dead!' Wade shouted.

Clobes reached for his pistol and Wade wasted another shell over his head. Clobes never hesitated. The gun came up and fired twice at the sound confronting him. Wade jerked back behind the rock, then put his next round in the horse's head and saw it stumble and go down hard, slamming the rider to the ground.

Clobes yelled in pain, holding his left arm as he rolled to his feet, sent another shot at Wade, and stood and ran for the nearest large boulder. Wade pulled up the Spencer, aimed low and fired. He watched the big slug take Clobes in the left thigh, blow the leg out from under him, and jolt the killer to the ground. His six-gun came out of his hand and fell six feet away. Clobes looked behind him and started to crawl toward the weapon.

'Give up up, Clobes,' Wade said and sent a round between the man and his gun, but he kept crawling toward it.

Wade came out of the cover and ran to the spot, picking up the six-gun, then turning toward Clobes.

'So what the hell, you caught me. My lawyer will get me off easy.'

'Not this time, Clobes. The old lady will testify against you. You killed her man, and she knew you were in that other room. You might as well have me blow a hole through your head right here as to bet on not hanging.'

Wade patted his pockets and his armpits but found no other weapons on Clobes.

'You aim to walk back to Prescott?' Wade asked him.

'Hell no.'

'Then why did you make me shoot your horse?'

Wade checked the hip wound. It had dug in hard and was still in the leg somewhere.

'Get me to a doctor, I need a doctor, Chisholm. This leg is hurt bad.'

'You giving orders now, killer? Go ahead, walk back to Prescott.'

Wade brought his horse from where he had tied it, and despite Clobes' screams, forked his legs over the back of the mount. 'Hang on to the saddle, big killer. I'm going to tie your feet together under her belly.'

'No, that'll hurt like hell. I can't go nowhere,' Clobes said.

'Damn right, nowhere but to the gallows.'

It was slow going, as the double loaded mount worked back down the trail toward Prescott. Chisholm had pushed his six-gun into the belt in front of him and unloaded the rifle, to give Clobes no chance at a weapon. They rode for an hour before Wade saw the posse riding up the trail.

He stopped and waited for them.

Marshal Logan was in front of the pack. He waved as he recognized Wade and pulled the group of ten men up in front of him.

'See you caught yourself a polecat there, Wade,' the marshal said.

'More like a skunk that works as bad as a sidewinder, Marshal. Wish you'd brought an extra horse.'

'Peers like that mount of yours has some staying power, let's give it a try and we can trade off. Any chance he might die on the way in?'

Wade shook his head. 'I tried to get it to bleed more, but the blamed thing keeps clotting up.'

Marvin Clobes could only scowl at the people. How did he know his deaf old uncle was such a favorite in this hick town?

*   *   *

They rode into Prescott just before one o'clock in the afternoon and fifty people were at the jail waiting for them. It wasn't a lynch mob, but there was no love for the killer either.

'How long we got to wait for the hanging, Marshal,' a man called from the front of the crowd.

'Man is innocent until we prove him guilty,' the Marshal said. Then he winked. 'Judge should be here in two weeks.

140

Shouldn't take long after that.'

Wade had arranged with the marshal that he would be back for the trial. Now he rode on through town to the Pony Soldiers at Camp Prescott.

General Crook was having lunch when Wade arrived and he was shown into the commander's private quarters.

'Understand you had some excitement,' Crook said.

'Word travels fast. How are my people on the reservation?'

'Only been there a few days. Last report I had they were settling down, getting used to the land. Unhappy about the lack of game, but I've arranged for them to have some wild steers that some of my boys rounded up. Figure they could breed up a herd if they halfway tried. Been thinking about irrigation. You know anything about spreading water out where it's needed?'

'Not much, General, not much at all.'

'Should learn. The Apache are going to become the best farmers in the whole Indian world.'

'How's that, General?'

'I'm going to teach them how to do it. And if you got any sense, you'd take a pair of gold oak leaves and help me.'

Wade laughed, and picked a chicken leg off the platter when the general offered it.

'I can still help you. Whenever you have a

project over at San Carlos, you give me a shout. I'm closer to them than you are. I just hope that you give the men something to do they can feel proud doing. We're a proud race, we Apaches, and digging in the ground has been woman's work for centuries.'

'Hunting beef, breeding up a beef herd, that could be man's work,' General Crook said.

'I hope the Apaches feel that way.'

The general twirled the twin points of his salt and pepper beard. 'I hear you have a new name now, Man In Two Camps. I like it. It fits you. I hope it will mean you give the Apaches the best of both camps.'

'I aim to, General. I surely do aim to.' He stood, then put the chicken bone back on the plate. 'General, I've got another project in the works. If I could be excused, I should be riding back to Phoenix.'

General George F. Crook nodded, took a pair of major's golden oak leaves from his vest pocket and looked at them. He shrugged and put them back in the pocket and reached for another piece of chicken as Wade left.

CHAPTER ELEVEN

BASKET FULL OF DREAMS

Wade had arrived in Phoenix the night before, had slept for ten hours in a real bed in the hotel, and had breakfast. He hadn't talked to Josh McCurdy yet. He walked down the street to the bank, cut across and stepped up on the boardwalk in front of a new office with the name of 'J. Lawson Ambrose, Attorney at Law,' printed on the small sign outside. Wade pushed the door open and walked inside.

Ambrose looked up and at once, stood from where he had been seated at his desk and took a step backward.

'Now don't get violent, Chisholm. I swear I never told that hothead to come after you in the hotel. He did that on his own, and I don't blame you for being furious, but that's not my fault. If you strike me I'll sue you for assault and battery, do you understand that?'

Wade sat down beside the desk, opened a humidor and took out a long cigar which he snipped the end off, then lit and leaned back, puffing esily.

'What hothead?' he asked.

'Oh, I thought you might be . . .'

'Upset because your client tried to kill me?'

143

'Well . . . yes. And I am getting ready to file a suit against you.'

'Who for? Who's the client?'

'Why, you know. Marvin Clobes Miller.'

'Marvin Clobes Miller. Well, interesting.' Wade tried three times to blow a perfect smoke ring, finally gave up. 'You think you have a client named Marvin Clobes?'

'I most certainly do, and you can't frighten me into quitting him. The poor man deserves that inheritance, and I'm determined to get it for him.'

'Half of it.'

'I beg your pardon?'

'You are determined to split it fifty-fifty, right?'

'Well, there always is a fee arrangement, you wouldn't understand that sort of thing.'

'Probably not. I do understand sharing though. If you're going to share with Clobes, I think you should share it all, right?'

'We do have an arrangement, anything else would be a violation of the client/lawyer relationship.'

'Good, I'll go for the fifty-fifty. Only how can a gent be half dead?'

'I beg your pardon?'

'I said, how can a gent be half dead?'

'I really don't understand what this gibberish is you're speaking.'

'I didn't think so. If you want a client you better get up to Prescott and defend one

144

Marvin Clobes against a charge of murder. Three days ago he shot down his 76-year-old uncle, whose last name is Clobes, and who had told me that the Clobes in these parts are not now and never have been any kin in any manner with the Millers of Phoenix. Just for the record. Just thought you'd like to know.'

Wade got up, and headed for the door.

'Wait a minute. You're telling me Clobes shot and killed his uncle, three days ago, in Prescott.'

'True.'

'Were there any witnesses?'

'Yep, two. Me, and the man's wife.'

'Oh, Lord!'

'True. He's got about as much chance of beating a murder charge as you do of talking a circuit court judge into giving you an injunction stopping the Hannah Miller School. So you'll have a one hell of a time trying to win a case for a dead man. Oh, did you know that the circuit court judge goes to Prescott, then comes down here. He'll have just sentenced Marvin Clobes to be hanged. Won't that be dandy for your suit?'

J. Lawson Ambrose stood and stared at Wade. 'Is this all true, or is it just a pack of lies to slow down my work on the case.'

'Ask anybody on the stage. It just got in ten minutes ago from Prescott. About half a day late, don't ask me why. Well, you have an interesting morning now, Mr. Ambrose. And

I should tell you that all of the legal business for the Hannah Miller School will be handled by our new lawyer Handsome Jones.' Wade got up and went to the door. 'Thanks for the cigar,' he said and walked outside.

Wade was half a block beyond the office when he saw Ambrose come out and walk quickly toward the stage office. Willy would have all the news, he always knew what went on at both Prescott and Flag after the stage arrived. Wade grinned and walked on toward Josh McCurdy's store.

Inside the merchant was busy. Wade grabbed a prune from the barrel, chewed the pit out and worked on the job of moistening up the dried fruit. He was almost to the point where it could be eaten when Josh looked up.

'That'll be a nickel for the prune, stranger,' he said gruffly.

Wade turned and tossed a new dime on the counter.

'What kept you? Heard you got in town last night.'

'Business,' Wade said.

'Consarnit, Wade! Tell me what you been up to 'fore I bust a gut here.'

Quickly Wade filled in the merchant on what happened on the trail, at the house in Prescott and on the Flag trail.

'So what were you doing talking to J. Ambrose?'

'You're sneaky, Josh, did I ever tell you

that? I told him his client was going to be dead in about three weeks. It's my hunch that he'll hightail it right out of that skunk's corner and we don't have to worry about a phoney claim against the foundation.'

Josh beamed. 'Now that's what I'd call good news.'

'Should be. What about Kleen? How's he coming along with those drawings? When can I look at things?'

'Anytime you want. They should have the foundations dug by now on that piece of ground closest to town we looked at. While you been off galavanting around, some of us on the board have been working.'

'Got the land for our price?'

'Right.'

'Kleen got the drawings done and has the foundations working?'

'True.'

'Find the adobe nearby?'

'Right at the edge of the river. We've got a crew and made over a hundred adobe blocks for a test.'

'Josh, I'd say you two have sure been busy. Where is Kleen, out at the site?'

'Has been for the past few days. I'd say he'd be there now.'

'So that's where I'm going.'

Wade rode out to the school site and swung down. Kleen was fitting a form into the just dug foot-deep footings, shaking his head at the man with the shovel.

'Look, there's no way we can squeeze down those adobe. You don't dig the hole big enough, we have to wait while somebody else digs it bigger. Make it a good job the first time, and everybody will be happier.'

Wade swung down and nodded to the feisty little builder.

'Morning, Mr. Kleen. Looks like your project is coming along just fine.'

'Legal problems?'

'I don't think we have a thing to worry about, Mr. Kleen. The litigant has just been charged with murder in Prescott, and with any luck he'll be hung dead in three weeks.'

'Oh, I didn't know. Is he guilty?'

'Guilty as hell.'

'Good. Good! Now if you'll excuse me . . .'

He strode off and checked on the line one of the foundation ditches was taking. A half hour later he paused and explained the system.

'We could use concrete footings, but I figure that would cost too much and the mortar and adobe should work just as well. These blocks are sixteen inches long, by four inches thick and twelve inches high. They can be any size. We'll use enough straw in them so they bind well, and put them in the foundation hole to start the foundations. Down here it will be two feet thick, then the wall will slope gradually until at the top of the

148

second story it will be only 12 inches wide.'

'Warm in winter, cool in the summer,' Wade said.

'True, but the adobe does have a special odor. I hope to plaster the inside of every room with honest to goodness plaster, which should relieve the strange musty odor.'

'Interesting, Mr. Kleen, do you have enough money? Are there any supplies you need?'

'All taken care of, Mr. Chisholm. And I might add I'm happy as a kid with a new pony. It's a project I can really dig into! Between Josh McCurdy and I we're moving it along fine. There will be a holdup now on the adobe. We won't get as far along this winter as I had hoped, because the blocks won't dry. But we'll do as much as we can, God willing.'

He hurried off then to set something right at the block curing area, and Wade sat watching him a minute on his mount, then rode back to the store.

He suddenly felt like a Man In Two Camps. He was thinking about the Apaches at San Carlos reservation. How were they getting along? What were they doing? What would the men do?

Back at the store he bought three lariats, a new pair of leather gloves, and then asked Josh if he knew anybody who had a few heifers they might want to sell.

Josh eyed him sternly. 'What in tarnation

you planning to do, start yourself a cattle ranch?'

'Something like that, who's selling?'

It took him three days to set it up. In the end he drew out the rest of the cash he had in the bank and borrowed $40 from Josh against his next army pay. Then he was moving. He hired an ex-cowpoke from the Golden Dollar Saloon to help him and by sunup they had the six head of stock on the move. Five heifers and one good yearling bull made up the entire trail herd, and both men felt a little strange with such a small bunch. But Wade quickly put the thought away, as they drove the critters down the trail toward the Superstitions to the east, then on toward the pass.

He would take them into the reservation, and see that Chief One Horse Thunder had the start of his beef herd.

It took them a day longer than it should have, but when he came into the reservation, he conferred with the Indian agent, and found that there was only one place much good for grazing, and it was half a day's ride from where the Chiricahuas had built their little camp.

They drove the cattle to the camp, and Chief One Horse Thunder came out with a gleam in his eye. He knew at once what his friend had done and he made the usual Chiricahua greetings, then held out his right

150

hand for a handshake.

'You are learning fast, Chief One Horse Thunder,' Wade said. Then they went into his wickiup and they talked for two hours. He had already had the small herd of cattle taken to the grazing lands and sent two young bucks along to tend to them. The one cow was pampered and fed grass and hay every day, and was producing milk well. But the chief said there was nothing for the men to do.

Wade led him outside and took out the lariats from his saddle, and began twirling one, showing them how to throw it to catch a horse, or a cow.

'Chief, this is a game that is also work. This winter the braves and younger boys must learn how to throw the lariat, how to rope a horse and a cow. Soon all the braves will be cowboys, riding their own horses, herding their own beef, making their own food for the long winters.'

The chief listened and nodded. 'Yes, it will be good, but it will take several summers to build up a herd. Are there other animals we can raise, that will grow even when the soil will not make our corn grow?'

'Chickens!' Wade said. 'I should have thought of it before, chickens. They hatch in 21 days as I remember. Then in two months you have chicken to eat, and to lay eggs. Perfect. Where can we get some eggs to hatch?'

Wade was getting excited thinking about it. With a few hundred chickens a band could have meat and eggs all year round.

'Let me go talk to the agent. I've got a lot of work to do.' He rode back to the small headquarters building and talked with the agent, explaining what he was trying to do, getting permission to bring in anything he wanted to in the way of self-help items for the Chiricahuas. Including chickens, hogs, anything he could find.

As he rode back towards the pass he looked back at the land. The San Carlos River would have water in it some times, during the spring and into the summer. Irrigation, just as General Crook mentioned, would bring the needed water into areas where there was fertile soil. Ditching would do it. A horse and a ditching plow could do a lot. Braves with picks and shovels could work the rest.

Wade began getting excited about it as he rode back toward the pass and on toward Phoenix. Now he was really a Man In Two Camps. And he was going to do everything he could to make life productive and safe and worthwhile for the Chiricahuas on their new reservation.

He had a good idea that General Crook could be relied on for some unofficial help as well.

Wade Chisholm rode faster then. He was

152

eager to get back to Phoenix, to get his work going for the Indians, find some chickens, figure out how to hatch them in the fall and winter to build up a flock quicker.

Then there was the Hannah Miller School. It was moving along well. He could sit and watch it grow and remember the woman it was named for. He wished again that she could be here to watch it take shape.

Wade shook off the feeling of loss and moved toward Phoenix. The Man In Two Camps had two lifetimes of work to do.

Photoset, printed and bound in Great Britain by REDWOOD BURN LIMITED, Trowbridge, Wiltshire

M.E.